MW01041903

SORCERERS REBORN

EARTH

To: WENDY

RICHARD B.

Sorcerers Reborn
Copyright © 2020 by Richard B.

All rights reserved. No part of this publication may be
reproduced, distributed, or transmitted in any form or
by any means, including photocopying, recording, or
other electronic or mechanical methods, without the prior
written permission of the author, except in the case of
brief quotations embodied in critical reviews and certain
other non-commercial uses permitted by copyright law.

Tellwell Talent
www.tellwell.ca

ISBN
9798722584571 (Paperback)

DEDICATION

Thanks to Bill Kraemer from Community Futures
for believing in me when others didn't.

ACKNOWLEDGMENTS

My sisters Pat and Terry, my brother Dennis, and their families, for their support.

Writers Guild of Alberta for their manuscript reading service, which gave me constructive criticism that led me to knowledge I was lacking.

Kimmy Beach Editing for doing the first edit of my book and for helping me understand the editing process.

Community Futures for their support, helping me get this far.

To my friends for their support.

To the people from Tellwell who have helped me understand the complications of self-publishing.

Richard B.

CONTENTS

Part 1
A New Beginning

Part 2
Gathering the Flock

Part 3
Things Unexpected

PART 1

A NEW BEGINNING

CHAPTER 1

MIDNIGHT

He stepped under the overhang and leaning his canes against the wall, shook the snow from his jacket and backpack. Gathering his canes, he opened the door and entered. The games room was busy as it always was, people spending their rent money hoping to double it and losing everything trying. Kristen was cleaning a table and saw him coming. Kristen was the bar manager and usually worked the dayshift.

"You're out late DeWayne! Do you want a beer? The snow's coming down pretty hard out there. I can't believe it is only the fifth of September."

"I do, but not just one can, an old man can have a lapse in his memory now and then. A dozen beer, and it is going to be another blizzard I'm afraid. You are working late again I see."

"Linda's youngest has the flu so I am filling in for her tonight."

DeWayne paid for his purchase and Kristen helped him with his backpack.

"Are you going to be all right? Getting home I mean? The snow's coming down hard out there. I can call you a cab if you'd like." Kristen looked at the frail old man, a concerned look on her face.

DeWayne laughed. "It will take a cab an hour to get here, and I can be home in half that time. I will be fine; after all I have made this journey hundreds of times, but thanks for your concern."

Kristen watched DeWayne make his way toward the door, as she had in the past. It was like watching a tortoise making its way across a furrowed field, slow and not so steady. She liked DeWayne; he was interesting, he talked about his past, the books he had written, and the books he would probably never get around to writing. For his age, and discounting his obvious disabilities, he was mentally sound; however, he did have a stubborn air about him. She knew that he was not going to be around much longer, according to him, but he was still going strong in her mind.

DeWayne stepped outside and stopped. Maybe Kristen was right. It was snowing heavily now, and the streetlights were dim as a result. He would have to be careful. DeWayne walked slowly, not because of the snow, but because of his disabilities. He stopped for the fifth time, by the vacant lot. Only one more block to go. He thought he heard a sound—other than his own heavy breathing—and looked around. He listened and heard the sound again.

A weak and pitiful meow came from the direction of the vacant lot. DeWayne spotted a dark shape in the six-foot strip of real estate between the sidewalk and the fence struggling to rise in the snow. He looked at the cat, evaluated the situation, and made his decision. He walked the few steps into the deeper snow and, planting his canes in the snow on either side, lowered himself to his knees. Pain shot through his body, but as he had done many times before, he blocked it, and pushed it out of his mind.

"I could have looked the other way." He spoke his thought aloud. "But you have a right to live just as I do." DeWayne unzipped his old winter jacket enough to put the bundle of wet fur inside. It was a good thing he had lost so much weight. He struggled to his feet and stood for a minute to let the pain subside.

Riding up in the elevator, DeWayne wondered if this was such a good idea. He had canned food, and milk, so the cat wouldn't starve. DeWayne closed his door, took the cat out of his jacket and put it on the rug at the end of the hallway. He removed the backpack and shook the snow off his jacket before hanging it up.

He put all the beer into the fridge except one, which he opened and took to the table beside his favorite chair in the living room before scrutinizing the cat. As the snow clinging to its fur melted it resembled a drowned rat. DeWayne took a large towel and moved the chair he used while putting on boots closer to the cat. He leaned over, and putting the towel over the cat, lifted it into his lap.

He was surprised when the cat purred as he dried its fur, trying not to hurt the fragile-looking creature. The cat was big, with pointed ears that looked unusually large for a cat, with eyes the color of gold—a midnight-black oval slit down the center of each one—and a long tail. Its paws looked more like the paws of a jungle cat, wide and with large claws. DeWayne could not help shuddering at the thought of the damage those claws could do. But he couldn't figure out if it was male or female.

DeWayne prepared two bowls, one with salmon and milk in the other. He put one of his throw rugs close to the cat and placed the two bowls on it. The cat sniffed the contents of both bowls before digging in.

DeWayne watched TV; the cat had finished eating and appeared to be sleeping when he glanced over to check on it. He had never had time for a pet with his work schedule. He had worked long hours with few days off right up until he got sick. Finding this stray right now wasn't what either of them needed. He was on his last legs, so to speak, and didn't have the right to get involved with an animal that needed a real home. The cat deserved a better place to live than DeWayne could offer. He would call the animal rescue folks in the morning and have them come and get it.

DeWayne put his empty beer can in the kitchen and went to bed. His mind was not willing to quit working though. Frustrated he got up and grabbed another beer. There was enough light coming from outside, even with the blowing snow obscuring most of it, so he didn't turn a light on. He glanced in the cat's direction every couple of minutes as he sipped, then he went back to bed once more.

The cat felt his frustration. She knew that she should wait, let him get used to her being around. But if he tried to get rid of her as he was thinking of doing, she would have to do something. She had to prepare him for what was to come, and for that he needed sleep. She could help him with that, and she could give him what would seem like a dream.

She closed her eyes and concentrated, shutting down DeWayne's thoughts one by one until he was calm and relaxed. With a thought she put DeWayne into a deep sleep. She jumped onto the bed and pressed her wet nose against his hand for a second, then she turned and jumped back down to the floor. She sat by the bedroom door and narrated the picture show with her vivid memory of those events.

<Thousands of years ago, on our world called Orighen, a Sorcerer named Tay'Ron, from the southernmost continent, decided that he wanted to rule our world. Of course, the rest of Orighen wasn't going to let that happen, so a long war was waged; one that lasted over five hundred years. Jakiera, the Queen of Geldania, a continent just above Orighen's equator, was a fair and just ruler. Geldania also had the most powerful army of all the continents: the largest army and more Sorcerers who were battle-ready. The southern tyrant, Tay'Ron, was intent on conquering the world, and making the people from the other countries bow down to him. Jakiera, and the other queens and kings of Orighen banded together to stop him. Jakiera also played a part in recruiting hundreds of dragons and elves to aid in this war.

<Over time, the opposing armies of Orighen finally drove Tay'Ron back to the southern continent. Six Sorcerers, a Furl Cat called Midnight, and a dragon called Scarlet brought Tay'Ron

to his end. Tay'Ron was a powerful Sorcerer and with his dying breaths he sent the six Sorcerers, and Midnight, to this world. The seven of them had no idea what happened to Scarlet. They arrived on an island to the west of here almost three thousand years ago. At first, they had no idea what was going on, or where they were. They did figure out that they were no longer on Orighen because nothing looked the same: plants, flowers, and animals were not from Geldania or Orighen. Nothing looked familiar, and they had no idea how they came to be where they were, wherever that was.

<They had their weapons, so food was not a problem. With the gift they could discern what was edible or not when it came to vegetables and greens. They utilized whatever they found to survive. It wasn't until several years later that they discovered Tay'Ron had also given them an incurable virus. But that story is for another day.>

———•००﴾◉﴿००•———

DeWayne woke up lightheaded and lethargic, like he would be waking up after taking a sleeping pill or drinking too many beers. He felt like he had slept forever, and not at all. He was relaxed and didn't have the discomforts he usually had when he woke.

He swung his legs over the side of the bed and sat thinking about the dream, the sluggishness leaving him. It was so realistic he could not seem to get it out of his mind, and that bothered him because any dreams he had in the past were forgotten minutes after he awoke. It was like someone telling a story and he was a part of that story; he remembered the details.

He wondered why he was feeling so much better than he usually did—another mystery he supposed. As he walked to the kitchen he looked at the cat, sitting on the rug, looking back at him.

"I suppose you're hungry. I will fix you something in a few minutes. But first I need a cup of coffee to help me wake up completely. My brain is still a little foggy from sleep."

DeWayne fixed a cup of coffee, then put milk in one clean bowl and a can of flaked chicken in another and set them down. He sat in his chair and watched the morning news and weather. When the cat was finished with its meal it sat under the TV watching him. For a moment, he wondered if the cat in the dream was the same one looking at him now, but that was foolish...or was it?

DeWayne looked outside and saw that the sun was out and the snow was melting so he decided to go shopping and do his other daily routines. The cat was waiting for him when he walked back in the door. He felt a bit uncomfortable with the cat staring at him like that. Its golden eyes seemed to look right through him.

"You had something to eat a couple of hours ago, so I know you're not hungry, maybe you have decided to go outside and relieve yourself. Damn it, do you even know what I am saying you confounded cat?"

The cat looked at him, as if it was wondering what kind of fool had rescued it. DeWayne shook his head, picked up the backpack and put the groceries away, took a beer out of the fridge and sat down.

Midnight looked at DeWayne. She was getting anxious, she knew she should give him more time, but she was beside herself with worry, so she blurted it out.

<You are dying, DeWayne Richards, as I too am dying. My time, like yours, is running out. Will you hear my story?>

DeWayne looked at the cat, almost dropping his beer as he jumped. The voice seemed to be female, like the voice in the dream.

"I must have drunk more beer than I remember. I'm hearing things, or at least I am imagining I'm hearing voices."

<There is nothing wrong with your hearing, DeWayne; I am speaking to you telepathically. Everyone knows cats can't talk, and I don't believe you are all that drunk, yet.>

DeWayne finished his beer in one gulp while looking at the cat; he looked at the empty can and went to the kitchen for another. As he sat down, he realized he was gawking at the cat.

"Maybe I'm going crazy, or maybe I'm dreaming, or maybe it's a combination of the two."

<I am called Midnight. I am a female of my kind, and I mean you no harm! Will you listen to my story or not?>

"I have to think about this for a while. Maybe, after I have had time to process this, and have a beer, or four, or maybe six, I will realize that all this was only a dream," DeWayne said, more to himself than the cat.

Midnight just sat there. She didn't say anything else—if she'd said anything to begin with. DeWayne's mind went back to the dream. Maybe if he wrote it down he could put what happened and the dream out of his mind. He sat at his computer and typed the dream as he remembered it, word for word, describing the images as close to real as words could paint the pictures.

There was no way to verify anything this cat who called herself Midnight said. He had no idea if this Orighen even existed. Even if it was a world that scientists had found, that's probably not what it would be called. It would be called Planet 1451 or something. He still had no reason to believe that any of this was real. DeWayne was frustrated. The cat hadn't spoken to him again; so, he was leaning toward the fact that it was probably another dream. Day dreaming was quite common.

"She said it herself, 'cats can't talk!'" DeWayne laughed at those words. Was he really buying this bullshit? He took his glasses off and rubbed his eyes. He read the words from his dream again. *Maybe he could save these pages and use it to write another book.* DeWayne chuckled at the thought. It had been almost twenty years since he wrote his last book, but it wouldn't be that hard. The only problem was that he wasn't going live long enough to finish it.

DeWayne turned his computer off and laid down for his afternoon nap. Because of his lung disease, the fluid his lungs produced made it hard for him to breathe, which woke him up on a regular basis. He stretched out on the bed, but sleep did not come. He tossed and turned, but he could not stop thinking about the cat. Was any of this real? Could this Midnight be from another world, and what did she want with him anyway? Frustrated with not being able to sleep, and not being able to think of anything else, he got out of bed and went for another beer. The cat was still sitting there, watching him. He went back to his bedroom, beer in hand.

Midnight sensed his discomfort. *Until he can believe in the possibility that what I am saying is true, I cannot help him. I don't know what I can do to show him I am telling him the truth. Unless...I show him my magic, let him see that it is real, that he is not imagining all of this.*

She turned away. Midnight knew she was getting weaker and her time was running out. Of course, time to her wasn't the same as it would be for someone who hadn't already lived for over ten thousand years. She would let him struggle with his thoughts for now. She sat down in front of the fridge. The door opened and she looked inside.

He likes his beer, so that is what I will do.

When DeWayne came out of the bedroom she was sitting in front of the fridge. DeWayne's thoughts were still scrambled but the cat was his responsibility now regardless of the situation.

"You must be hungry. I'll fix you something to eat."

DeWayne opened a can of flaked chicken, put that in a bowl, and he put milk in another. When she finished her meal, she sat in front of him while he watched TV in the living room. He tipped his can of beer up to drain it.

<Let me do that for you,> she said before he could get up to get another.

A can of beer began to materialize on the table beside the empty can, right before his eyes. DeWayne swallowed hard, as he looked at the unopened can. He picked it up, opened it and took a drink, hoping it wasn't going to kill him. It was like the beer he bought from the store.

"How did you do that?" he asked, eyes wide.

<I am a creature of magic. Magic gives me the ability to create whatever I can imagine, something no one else on Earth can do at this time. Now I will ask you again: will you listen to my story?>

DeWayne looked at her for a long time, trying to keep his wits about him. *I cannot explain how she did that, or why she is showing me that she really does have magic. A little bit of excitement in this otherwise drab life of mine might be welcome, so why not?* It wasn't as if he was going anywhere, and she was right: he was on his last legs, so he didn't have anything to lose.

"First, I want to know something. Was that you in the dream I had last night? Was that your doing?"

A shadow formed around Midnight, growing to become an outline of the large cat from the dream. DeWayne swallowed hard.

"Okay, Midnight, that was a little dramatic. You asked me if I would listen to you. I am not saying that I am convinced, but you have my interest. Tell me your story."

<Very well. Our story begins on my home world, Orighen.>

The start of Midnight's story was exactly like the dream; however, he did not interrupt her.

<Now I will tell you of my time here on this world. I understand that what you hear may not be easy for you to understand or believe. For now, all you need to know is that I am the only one left to speak for the others who were lost. As my friends died, I was able to take each gift of sorcery into myself, being a Furl Cat, and store each of them individually.

<I have chosen five already and given them each their gift; now I have only one left. I have been watching you on and off for the past ten years, DeWayne, and I have decided that you are more than worthy of this honor. Will you allow me to give you the last gift of sorcery that I carry?>

Again, DeWayne was taken aback at the cat's words. He took his glasses off and rubbed his face. He wasn't dreaming. It was she who gave him the dream. What was this gift she was talking about giving him, and how the hell was any of this even possible?

<The gift will allow you to live past the life of the body you have now. I will teach you all I can about how to use the gift before I die. How long I have left I cannot say, but if I use my gift sparingly maybe I will get to teach you enough.>

"I don't understand. I have already lived longer than they said I would. I have maybe six more months left to live."

Midnight shook her head slowly.

<When I give you the gift of sorcery, your body will have the power to heal itself. However, you are going to have to let this you die. You will have to adopt another identity, another you. I know it isn't easy to understand right now, but you must realize it is the only way. Once you have the gift, I can keep your body the same as it is now, with all your medical issues as they are today, but without the pain you suffer now.

<You must see that this you must die. It all starts with you accepting the gift. We can work on the rest of the details once you complete the transition from mortal to Sorcerer. Do you understand what I am telling you?

<One more thing: once you accept my offer, there is no turning back. I cannot reverse the process, so think this over, and make sure you're ready.>

DeWayne took his glasses off and closed his eyes. Again, he raised his hands to his face, going over everything Midnight had said.

He got up and grabbed another beer. He had always believed that there had to be other planets out there that could sustain life. Was this proof that there were other inhabited planets with sentient beings on them, or was this still a bad dream? He only had a short time left to live, and he had wondered what it would be like to have the knowledge he had now with the chance of another life. It had seemed a foolish dream. He turned what she said over in his mind, sifting through his thoughts as a gambler does before he rolls the dice and kept coming up with snake eyes. Gambling was like that: you had to be willing to take a chance, even when it seemed your luck had run out.

DeWayne shook his head, trying to think of a reason not to accept Midnight's offer, but he came up short. He stood in front of the window. *Dr. Hanson told me that the results from the MRI were not good, just three days ago. She said I most likely was not going to make it another six months. Mind you she has been saying that for the past ten years. But I know she is right; I don't need the tests to tell me the lung damage is getting worse. Now I have a choice to make, do I accept this gift Midnight is talking about and live for God knows how much longer, or do I refuse and die within six months. I am not ready to die.*

He looked at Midnight. "I have questions: first, did you have something to do with me living as long as I have? You did say you have been watching me on and off for the past ten years. Also, it seems that all I have to do is to think of what I want to say and you know what I am thinking. Are you reading my mind?"

Midnight nodded.

So, living this long hasn't been sheer luck, it was magic. How am I supposed to die, but not die? Why am I able to communicate with her? How long will I live with this gift?

What Midnight was saying, seemed to be too good to be true. If it sounded too good, then the chances are it was. DeWayne looked at her for a long time before responding. It was only a few hours ago that he went out to get more beer, found a stray cat, and bought it home. Now he was sitting here talking to that cat and trying to decide if he was going to accept this gift she was offering him. DeWayne weighed everything Midnight had told him. Everything from the bloody war, to the friends she had lost, to right now, sitting here with him.

He couldn't believe that he was considering this. Did he want to live another lifetime? Could he afford to live another lifetime, the length of which was undecided? He was in constant pain, from the tip of his toes to the top of his hair, and breathing was like trying to suck air though a folded paper napkin. Dying would be the end of all that, but, was he ready to die?

"All right. I have often wondered what my life would be like if I could start over, and still know what I know today, and reading other people's minds would be a bonus. Let's do this; as you said earlier, we can work the rest out later. If we don't do this now, I might change my mind. How do we begin?"

Midnight looked at DeWayne, tilting her head from side to side, as if she was sizing him up for a new suit, or her next meal.

<I am a creature of magic, created by magic; therefore, the rules of sorcery do not apply to me. You will be a Sorcerer, and you will not be able to read other people's minds. It's against the rules of sorcery, rules that you will learn first before anything else. You will be able to speak telepathically to other Sorcerers. Your other questions will be answered in time. You need to eat a good meal first, and you should have food ready for after, when your recovery begins. I believe this will take a lot of energy, and you should be prepared. I am not sure what is going to happen, because I have never done this before.>

DeWayne's eyes widened, again. "I thought you gave the gift to five others," he said. "What do you mean you're not sure what's going to happen? Am I your lab rat, so you can use me as your test subject?"

Midnight sighed. < I did not activate the gift in the others, I only transferred the gift to them. The gift in them is still dormant. You will be the first one I give the gift to with it already active. I will teach you as much as I can so you can teach the others when they come. And they will come.>

DeWayne shook his head. *What am I getting myself into here? This sounds like one of those TV ads, 'Get it now, this is a limited time offer.'*

"All right. Let's do this! I don't have anything to lose, except maybe my last six months."

He ate what he could and had food ready in the fridge for later. Midnight suggested that he lie down, saying it would be easier for him. Midnight sat beside him on the bed and pressed a paw to his cheek. At first, nothing seemed to be happening. Then suddenly, images and flashes of light raced through his mind, so fast that he lost all concept of time. Everything blurred into a scrambled mass of nothing, and everything. He didn't black out until it was done doing whatever it was doing.

DeWayne came around, his mind reeling and his body aching. He lay there for a long time, it seemed. He did feel different: more alive, maybe even as if he had been reborn.

<You should eat to replenish your energy! Come on! Get up, move around, and eat something. It will help you to recover.>

DeWayne struggled to rise, finally putting both feet on the floor and pushing himself into a standing position, then slowly putting one foot in front of the other until he made his way to the kitchen.

<I sense that you are going to have to touch the gift inside you, to become one with it, to make it a part of you. It is there, I can see it, but it is not connected to you. Right now though, you need to eat, and rest. You will have to keep to your daily routine, whatever it is: shopping, going for a beer, the things that you do every day, so no one notices anything different.>

DeWayne held his hands up. "Slow down my friend, I need to recuperate first. How long was I out? Am I a Sorcerer? My canes are still in the bedroom."

She looked up at him. <I am sorry if it seems like I am in a rush, but I don't know how much time I have left, and no you are not a Sorcerer yet. You have to make the gift a part of you, and you were out about twelve hours.>

DeWayne nodded and continued eating. He was hungry. As his energy returned he asked Midnight, "You said I had to touch the gift inside. What does that mean exactly?"

Midnight looked at him, shook her head.

<I'm not sure DeWayne; I just feel it is something you must do. You were not born with the gift, like the Sorcerers I came here with so long ago. As I said, I can see it. How you do that, I cannot help you; that is something I know nothing about. Your first lesson I suppose.>

When he was done eating, he lay down trying to think of what he needed to do to touch this gift. Midnight jumped up on the bed and sat down. He searched his memory looking for a process that would help him with completing the transition to Sorcerer. DeWayne settled on meditation. He had read somewhere that meditation helped one connect with one's inner self and he already used it to ease his pain. He drifted deeper into his subconscious mind, until he saw a tiny blue light, a small spark.

It was no bigger than the head of a pin. He reached out to touch it, but it seemed to move out of reach. He had been in the trades most of his adult life, so he analyzed the situation, and he thought for a minute before trying again. This time he moved to surround it, and gently closed in on it from all directions, until he was able to hold it with his mind. A shock wave spread outward from that tiny blue speck, and coursed through his body, making it tingle from the tips of his toes to the top of his hair. The shock was slight, but he felt it move throughout his body until it had engulfed him. DeWayne could feel the difference. He felt more alive, more so than he had after he woke up, and more than he had for the past thirty years.

Midnight let out a long sigh, sensing that DeWayne had succeeded, and they both slept for a time.

DeWayne woke and got dressed. There was shopping to do. If he was going to have to eat five or six meals a day to keep his body in shape, he needed more proteins, carbs, and vitamins. It looked like a reasonably nice day. The sun was shining and there were large fluffy cumulus clouds making their way across the sky. DeWayne made a list and looking it over decided to take his two-wheeled grocery cart, as well as his backpack. It was a long list. He looked at Midnight.

"I will be gone for a couple of hours, because I can only move so fast at the best of times, and then there's this cart, and I'll have to stop to catch my breath a few times as well, and of course I have to stop for my beer. You did say that I have to keep to my routine."

<We will start your first lesson when you return, and after you've had time to rest,> Midnight said.

As DeWayne started walking, he realized the pain he normally felt was not as prevalent as it had been; however, he still had problems breathing even with the added oxygen. He picked his pace up a bit, but only a little because he traveled this same route all the time and people might notice if he was moving faster than normal. When he arrived at the grocery store, he used a shopping cart inside with his cart folded up hanging on the side. DeWayne wasn't looking for deals, but he found that most of the items on his list were for sale. *A bonus.* He didn't want to overdo it, so he only took what he needed for a couple of days.

The woman at the checkout smiled. "That's more than your usual haul. Expecting guests?"

"Winter is here early again, and I do have a freezer at home. There will be days that I won't be able to get out because of the weather, so I am making sure there is enough, in case of emergencies."

The load was heavier than he expected, so by the time he arrived at the bar, he was trying to catch his breath. The pain was barely noticeable, but his breathing was a different story.

DeWayne sat at his usual table, drinking his usual beer of choice, and talked with Kristen. When DeWayne left the bar he was rested enough to make it the rest of the way home without too many stops.

Midnight watched him as he put the groceries away. DeWayne felt his age. When he was finished, he opened a beer and sat down for a while before they started his first lesson.

"I thought you said I wouldn't be the way I was after becoming a Sorcerer. I am out of breath, but I don't feel the pain as much."

Midnight looked at him.

<Drink your beer, lesson, and then we can discuss your concerns.>

DeWayne didn't argue with her as he sipped his beer then dozed in his chair. An hour later Midnight sat in front of him.

<Now that you're rested, I will give you your first lesson. Hold your hand out.>

DeWayne did so, and Midnight touched it with her wet nose. Images and words in a language he did not recognize at first filled his mind. His memory told him he did know, and understand, the hieroglyphic-like symbols. He sipped his beer as he took the information in. These were the rules Midnight had mentioned. Reading another's mind was not necessary, one could glean all the information from another's action, reactions, body language, and facial expressions. The rules were basic and more common sense than obstructive.

"What language is that? Why can I understand it?"

<It is the language of Orighen. The gift I gave you is from there so now that it is a part of you, you can understand. However, the others will understand it when they see it as well. Now, I want you to study that can of beer you're holding; see it with your mind. See everything it contains, everything that goes into that brew, all the separate ingredients. See how it all comes together to make your beer. Then I want you to study the can, and see what it is made of, and do the same with it, then reproduce your beer exactly, can and all.>

DeWayne thought about what Midnight had said and decided that if he went to the brewer's website, he could find out what components went into their beer, but he doubted they would list the portions for each ingredient. The can was made from an aluminum alloy, and he had a working knowledge of metallurgy, so he shouldn't have a problem with that part.

It took DeWayne several hours, and multiple failures trying to get the brew exactly right. He stopped long enough to eat something, before going back at it. DeWayne worked on trying to reproduce his can full of beer most of the night; he was surprised at how hard it was to get it even close to being right. He finally accomplished his task in the wee hours of the morning—a can, full of drinkable beer.

Chilling the beer took quite a bit longer though. First, he had to figure out how to cool the beer, and that took him a whole day. Once he figured that out, he had to fine-tune the temperature, so he was not freezing the liquid. He thawed a few cans out enough before he could drink them. In this one lesson he learned several aspects of the magic he had to employ to reach the desired end.

DeWayne took a break before Midnight touched his hand with her nose and showed him his next task: to take a tomato and start working on reproducing that. This task was much harder than the can of beer because he didn't have a list of ingredients as a starting point. He tried to picture the tomato in his mind, but he was not seeing the whole picture. It did not seem to matter how he thought he saw it, his tomato was far from being a tomato, and as far away from being edible.

This is going to take forever.

DeWayne was frustrated with his repeated failures. Making an edible tomato was a wake-up call; it was the way he was thinking. It was taking far too long. Midnight was not helping him at all.

<This is something you need to learn by yourself. If I help you, you are not going to learn; you're going to do as I say. It is up to you to SEE what you are looking at, so you understand what elements make a tomato, and how to reproduce it on your own. You must learn how to use the magic without anyone showing you how. Otherwise, you will always have to depend on someone else to help you, and that is not acceptable. Learn from your mistakes, make your mistakes work for you, and learn why it is not working.>

CHAPTER 2

A NEW BEGINNING

As DeWayne finished one task, Midnight gave him another—each one more complicated than the last. He was getting better at seeing what he had to see to get the results he was aiming for. Midnight let him know that she was pleased with his progress, but didn't make the lessons any easier for him.

<You have to understand that the more you use magic to accomplish these tasks that seem hard for you, the easier it will get. And that's when you can start experimenting for yourself; however, I will still be here watching to see that you don't blow yourself, or the apartment, up. One more thing you need to know. When you go out never use your magic. People don't understand it. There is no sense in advertising you have it.>

DeWayne felt like he was back in grade school with Mrs. Bell. She was always telling him he had to "Pay more attention young man! You cannot depend on others to do your homework for you. That's why you're here: to learn."

With the gift, he only needed to sleep for a few hours a day, waking refreshed. DeWayne spent a couple of hours every day working out in his apartment. He believed that getting, and staying, in shape had to be a part of his daily routine. Becoming a Sorcerer meant his ailments no longer held him back, but that didn't mean he could ignore his physical body. There was plenty of time to work out and go about his he usual routine of shopping and stopping for a beer, weather permitting, before Midnight's daily lesson. In between, DeWayne and Midnight talked about how they were going to accomplish the transformation from DeWayne to his new self.

Reading was going to be a big part of that. Magic enhanced his abilities to not only read faster, but also to retain what he was reading. With each page he improved, until after a few days he could glance at a page and remember everything on it. Knowledge of coding, hacking, and being able to delve into the darker side of the internet would be beneficial, and he had no trouble accomplishing that. Once he learned how to hack into other websites, the rest came easily enough.

DeWayne created a new identity. He chose the name Jason Blain, derived from two people from his past. Jason had been a close childhood friend who had died from cancer. Blain was the maiden name of his wife, the only woman he had ever loved, who had died in a car accident far too young. Both their losses had been hard for him to deal with.

As the weeks passed things moved much faster than DeWayne expected. Once he became a Sorcerer his whole being changed, his whole life changed. He only required a few hours' sleep, so he had twenty hours to do things he had to do and still learn from Midnight. DeWayne learned how to hack into government and bank websites to create his new identity online. He established accounts for Jason Blain, created the credit, banking, and other cards he would need. DeWayne's increasing ability to see things with his mind, allowed him to flawlessly create everything that was needed with magic. After three weeks of hard work that felt like three months Jason's identity was ready, complete with a driver's license, government ID, health care card, and a bank card. All that was left was a picture of his new self, Jason.

DeWayne had a new name and identity, but he needed a new face—to change himself from this old man into a younger, different self. Midnight explained that he had to be exact when changing every part of his body, inside and out. DeWayne made a sketch detailing height at 190 cm, weight at 91 kg, eye color blue as they were now, hair light brown, and skin color tanned, and Caucasian as he was. He could adjust the external details as he went. Like everything else, the process had challenges that he had to overcome. He understood Midnights insistence that he had to accept his new identity; after all, changing his appearance was not changing him, just how he looked. DeWayne was not sure he could do that yet.

<There is much more to do before you can become Jason for real,> Midnight had said. <Your new identity will aid you in acquiring the items you will need for your new life. When the time comes for DeWayne to leave this world, all our plans will have to be complete.>

"I can change how I look Midnight, but I cannot change who I am. I will always be DeWayne. Jason will be my alter ego, my outside persona, and DeWayne will still be me when I am in my own home."

<I don't think that is a wise choice; however, that is your decision to make,> she said.

He kept at it until he could change from one identity to the other in the time it took him to blink. Now that he had that part mastered, it was time to move on to other details of his changing life. He took a picture for his driver's license so he had picture ID.

He had been withdrawing a thousand dollars from DeWayne's account, three times a week, for the three weeks it had taken to get to this point. He kept it in a drawer for when he would move to a new apartment, after the death of who he was now. He could make bi-weekly deposits into Jason's account just like he was depositing a paycheck. The next tasks were to get a vehicle and an apartment for Jason. Because of his illnesses and mobility problems, DeWayne made a habit of checking in with the manager of his current apartment building on a regular basis to let her know he was okay. Now he told her he would be gone for two or three days to get some medical tests.

DeWayne packed a few clothes and toiletries for Jason into his backpack and left his apartment after sunset. He found a dark alley that would afford him the opportunity to transform into Jason without being noticed, and then changed his backpack into a suitcase. He walked to a hotel and booked a room for two nights; hopefully, that would be enough time to do everything he had to do. He had already researched cars and apartments, and had a couple of appointments set up.

—∘∘⟨◉⟩∘∘—

A young woman approached him as he entered the used car lot and showed him several cars in his stated price range. He wanted an older car with a specific fuel-cell system. She did have one older car with the fuel-cell system for producing electricity. It was a black, sporty looking car, so the bargaining began. Within an hour he had a car that ran reasonably well, and he could fix it up later if it were needed. The dealer put the plate on and Jason drove back to the hotel.

Jason had the buffet for lunch, which he visited three times, in the hotel dining room. With a full belly, he went to his first appointment for an apartment. Jason buzzed the manager. An older woman greeted him at the office door.

"Hi, I'm Betty the property manager. What are you looking for, a one or two bedroom?"

Jason shook her hand and said, "I am Jason Blain. I would like to see one of each before I decide."

She showed him a small unit on the fourth floor and then a corner apartment on the ninth floor. It was much nicer than the one DeWayne lived in now, and cheaper as well. It was a two bedroom, with a large master bedroom including an en suite bathroom. The kitchen was twice the size of the one he had now, and the living room was much bigger as well. It wasn't as if he needed the extra room, but he was not going to worry about that right now.

"I like what I see, and for the price you're asking, I'll take it!" Jason said.

When the paperwork was finished Jason went shopping. He bought everything cheap. However, he looked at the top-of the-line products of everything he bought so he could improve them if he wished. *The more you use your magic the better you will get.* He only took what would fit in the car; everything else would be delivered the next morning. After he unpacked the smaller items he took the laptop with him and put the boxes in the recycle bin as he left the building.

Back at the hotel he ordered from room service—T-bone steak with all the fixings—and used his gift to upgrade the laptop computer to a top-of-the-line of its kind while he waited for his meal to be delivered.

DeWayne hacked into the hospital he was sure he would be sent to and reviewed all of the information on their intensive care unit. He needed to know everything he could find out about how they ran that part of the hospital, so Midnight and he could finish putting their plan together.

The next morning he let the delivery people into the apartment with the furniture. DeWayne put the TV stand together by hand and hooked the TV to the cable and power outlets. The computer stand and computer came next. The bedroom and living room were simple and did not take long. It was late when he left the building, so he left the car there and took a cab back to the hotel.

———••◦◦❁◦◦••———

All the pieces were in place, it was time to end DeWayne's life and begin Jason Blain's. DeWayne had a moment of doubt as he considered what he was doing.

Midnight sensed his hesitation. <You have a will made out leaving everything to those you would leave behind. They too, know your time for dying is coming soon. You told your nieces and nephews so in a letter you sent them before you became a Sorcerer. If you don't die, and change your appearance, then people are going to start asking questions. After all you should have died years ago. You have lived much longer than anyone expected, including yourself, something I may have had a hand in. Let this life go and begin a new one.>

Midnight was right. This was the only way this could go.

Part of the plan required DeWayne to become invisible. Midnight showed him how it was supposed to work, and he spent hours trying to achieve that end.

"Midnight, I am having trouble here. Please, come here and show me what I am doing wrong, or at least tell me if I am getting closer."

Midnight looked at him as if she were looking right through him.

<Try it again. I will watch you closely this time; maybe I can show you what you're not doing right. Or I can tell you to keep on trying until you get it right. Which of those two options do you think I will choose?>

DeWayne had no illusions of what her choice would be and tried again. Midnight walked around him, studying him, as she would a bird or a mouse she was about to pounce on.

<This can't be right. Why did I not see this before? I don't understand how this could happen, DeWayne, but it appears that your gift of sorcery has been contaminated with my magic, and it has become a combination of both.

<I missed it. Everything I have showed you up to now has worked as it should have. The invisibility spell should have worked as well. I am going to have to rethink this. For now, I will show you how I turn invisible, and we will see if my analysis is correct.>

Midnight put one of her front paws on his arm, and he had a mental picture of what he was supposed to do. When he did as Midnight showed him, he vanished. He reappeared and looked at her.

"Did that work? I didn't feel anything," DeWayne said.

<It worked as it should DeWayne; now give me time to think this through. I have questions that I have no answers for.>

DeWayne watched Midnight jump up on her chair; he didn't know what to make of this either. He went into the bathroom and, standing in front of the full-length mirror on the back of the door, he tried vanishing again. He was a little unnerved when his reflection disappeared before his eyes. The vanity, toilet and bathtub were all visible in the mirror. Invisibility, according to what Midnight had first shown him, involved manipulating light and color, and blending it all in with the background.

Midnight watched DeWayne practice. She was sure that this mutation had been there from the first day she gave DeWayne the gift. She had not considered that having two kinds of magic— one being latent, the other fully operational—that one would somehow leach into the other, making a new form of magic. She had carried those six bundles of sorcery for over three thousand years. Midnight closed her eyes. *This means that the other five will be the same.*

She had all the knowledge of the Furl Cats, and nothing spoke to the time one could hold that magic inside. The only thing that she knew was that she could do what she did, taking the gift from one who was dying and give it to another who was alive.

Well, she thought, *there is nothing that I can do about it now, and I doubt that there ever was. My biggest problem is, do I tell the others when they come, or do I keep this to myself. I already carry enough secrets that will be revealed when the time is right. That is, I believe, for the best. I will see how things play out when the others arrive.*

DeWayne also had to be able to create an identical replica of himself, a golem with all his old injuries, diseases, and tattoos.

Any discrepancies, even the smallest, might be noticed if they did an autopsy. So DeWayne practiced. He studied his body with his gift. He started building the replica with the skeleton, then added organs, muscle, tissue, and skin. The fact that the human body was over 50% water helped. The first time took most of the day, but with each attempt it became that much easier and after five days he could do it in minutes.

It was the middle of October and it was time. DeWayne left as usual and did grocery shopping then went to the bar for his morning beer. He rose from his chair, made it look like he was having trouble standing up and getting his breath, before collapsing and knocking over the chair he was using for support. Kristen rushed over, yelling for someone to call 911. DeWayne slowed all his vital signs down and gave his skin a pale hue. The paramedics arrived soon after and recognized him from other calls. They loaded him into the ambulance, and sped off with sirens blaring.

The nurse in emergency recognized DeWayne, and after Doctor Hanson had examined him, he was sent to intensive care. Once they had all the fancy machines connected to him and everyone had left the room, he scanned every machine using his magic. DeWayne only had to wait until the nursing staff changed shifts, and he would have at least fifteen minutes to complete his tasks.

At the changing of the guard, DeWayne hacked the camera in his room to record a five-minute loop and set it to play on the monitors at the nurses' station. He got up, leaving all the leads to the machines connected and keeping his vitals constant. Using magic he created the golem and made the heart pump and lungs breath as they would in a living human.

He then attached all the leads to the replica, making the machines believe the body was alive. Then he transformed into Jason and vanished. The machines would keep working until he released them. DeWayne cancelled the video loop and left the room when a nurse came in to check on him. He waited by the main entrance for one of the nurses changing shifts and he followed her outside. Then he released the magic that kept the golem's heart working. DeWayne was dead. Jason moved to an alley to become visible, then pulled a hoody up to conceal his face and began the long walk to his new home.

Midnight was waiting for him, and everything he had wanted to keep from his old life had been transferred to the new apartment. *It isn't going to be easy looking in the mirror every day and seeing another face. I will have to get used to it, if that is possible,* he thought.

Over the next couple of days, DeWayne needed something different to occupy his mind. When he was younger he had dreamed of playing in a band; he also wanted to finish writing the books he had started so long ago. Work had always come first—putting food on the table was more important than playing music and spending days writing. When he retired, he did get to write, and published two of his books, but his arthritis was already too far gone to get into the music he still loved.

DeWayne liked to write and chose to start by writing a poem about his last twenty years. He scratched out a crude draft on a note pad, then he modified it line by line until he had a decent poem. Of course, this poem might never see the light of day, because Jason hadn't lived those twenty years, DeWayne had.

DeWayne realized he was going to have to put his name on hold; DeWayne was dead. But he was not dead, he was sitting right there at his computer, wearing a Jason disguise. No one was going to see him in his own apartment, and he could change into Jason before he opened the door. Jason changed back into DeWayne. He finished the poem and read it over.

"Till we meet again"

A life spent mostly in pain, but always a love of life
A wish for it all to end, but a stronger will to survive
When you have only one life to live
When you only have a short time left
You live that life to the fullest, doing all that you can
You live for every second, every hour, and every day
Life in pain is hard to live, but you gather your strength
Your love for Life, is the strength you need to carry on
To love the people you love most in life
To love your family, and friends
Your time has come my friend, to leave us
Your life in heaven, will smile down on us all
From the wings of an eagle
Till we meet again, in heaven my friend
When heaven calls

CHAPTER 3

FROM A DREAM

Midnight saw DeWayne reappear.

<You cannot change back into your old self. What if someone sees you?>

"The door is locked. No one can walk in here unannounced, Midnight. I am not Jason; he is my disguise when I am out there. In here, where no one can see me, I am DeWayne, and that is not going to change."

<I thought you had changed your mind. I am disappointed that you cannot accept your new life fully. Being Jason is a hard thing for you to deal with and I get that. When I came to this world I was myself: a large, foreign, Furl Cat. In order for me to fit in with this world's cats I had to change who I was. It took me years to come to terms with that, as it will take you time to accept Jason as who you are now. Right now, you're being selfish insisting that you're not going to change. DeWayne is dead and buried. How are you going to explain DeWayne to the others when they come? When they find out Jason isn't who they thought he was they will turn around and run. You could tell them your story if you chose to, but I highly suggest that you do not. If you insist on being stubborn, I will not argue your choice. However, I am not pleased with your decision.>

DeWayne watched her stomp down the hall. *She does this all the time, making me feel like a little kid in grade school. Maybe she is right, maybe I should reconsider my choices.*

"Thank you for that." He shouted as her tail disappeared around the corner.

"I am going to write a book. However, I have some studying to do first."

Things have changed since I last published. I have a new tool in my toolbox though. I can learn English literature, writing style, and self-editing online.

Understanding grammar, punctuation, and all the nuances of English literature took several days. Publishing could wait until he was ready for that part. From the time Midnight had first given him the gift, he had dreamed most nights of another world, fighting evil Sorcerers and their minions. When he asked Midnight about the dreams she said his gift of sorcery belonged to the Sorcerer Richard and that the sorcery was giving him these dreams from what it still had of his memories.

He decided to write his book using those dream-memories that he had documented on his computer. The only real writing would be connecting everything together to make the story complete. The main characters were eight Sorcerers, a Furl Cat, and a dragon. Midnight of course was the Furl Cat. DeWayne sat at his computer and began.

---∘∘⚬❋❁⚬∘∘---

THE BOOK

The Invasion of Geldania

It was overcast this night as I sat at the fire with five others eating our evening meal of stew, bread, and wine. We all needed some rest and nourishment before tonight's raid. We had been tracking the band of raiders from the southern continent for the past two days. It was hard to believe that we'd been battling bands of raiders for over sixteen winters.

I looked around at the rag-tag group, each wearing a loose-fitting tunic and leggings in an abstract pattern, with varying shades of browns, greens, and blacks. The loose garments gave us freedom of movement, and the patchy abstract pattern on our clothes offered a better chance that the enemy would have a difficult time seeing them. They were all armed with two swords, hilts showing over each shoulder, their straps crossing their chests. Their belts held both a long knife and two smaller ones. Some had throwing knives hidden in their clothes, others had bows on the ground by their feet.

We all had our reasons for being here. I had been out hunting with Bragg, from a neighboring farm, and we were dragging a small Kolten carcass home. As we came over the hilltop at sunset, I saw the tendrils of smoke in the distance. I still remember the sinking feeling in my gut. My home, Valaren Ranch, had been burned to the ground, bodies strewn across the green space in front of the main house and the roadway.

"I have to get home, Richard," Bragg said. "It looks like whoever did this was going that way. There is nothing we can do here, for now."

We ran as fast as we could to Chelsea Farm, but we were too late. Everyone there was dead also, and only blackened skeletons remained of the buildings. We buried the dead and marked each grave with pieces of wood, the name of the one buried there carved into each one, then repeated the process at Valaren Ranch.

"Bragg, go back and gather what you need. It is time we left. I am going to find those who did this and make them pay. If you want to join me, you are welcome to do so."

"I think I will go to my older brothers, and I hope they are still all right. You're a good friend, Richard; take care of yourself, till we meet again."

I haven't seen Bragg since. This group has become my family.

Liam, was my height of six metra two centra with light brown eyes and brown hair that reached halfway down his back, tied with three leather bands. His scruffy beard made him look like one of the southern raiders. Liam was easy-going regardless of the pain he had suffered when his wife, children, family, and friends had died at the hands of the southern invaders. He had been out fishing with others from the small village of Paltaren at the time.

Cheryl was the tallest of the women in the group at six metra tall. Her long dark brown hair, worn in a braid, matched her eyes. She had six throwing knives concealed in various places in her clothing, and she knew how to use them. Cheryl had been fifteen winters old and out hunting when she heard shouts and screams. She rushed toward the sounds, but arrived as the soldiers and Sorcerers were leaving Obed Village. Cheryl still had nightmares of that horrible day.

Joanne was the shortest of the women at five metra six centra tall with green eyes and long reddish-brown hair tied in a ponytail with leather bands. She remembered having to bury her parents, brother, and sister. The Sorcerers and their soldiers came in the early morning, balls of fire exploding against the walls of the houses, arrows flying through the air. Joanne had taken an arrow in her side and dropped to the ground, fainting from the pain. When she woke, she was the only one left alive. Joanne had only been ten winters old, but she recovered and joined us.

Pam stood five metra eleven centra tall, her cold, deep blue eyes, stared out from the long blond hair that hung to her shoulders, before it ended in a loose ponytail, which ran down her back to her waist. She had only been eight winters old when everyone in the hamlet of Farnsworth had been murdered by the southern soldiers. She had seen Tamara, her older sister, drop to her knees, an arrow protruding from her back. Pam ran for the forest. Once she had buried the dead and salvaged what she needed to survive, she left the only home she'd ever known.

Valla was as tall as Pam with red hair that reached to her waist, tied with bands of leather. She too, had only been eight winters old when tragedy struck her home. She had been picking berries with friends a metronome from the small town of Nora. When they returned there was little left standing. After they interred their dead and gathered what food and weapons they could find she sent her friends to Tannerville while she set out for revenge.

All six of us have our reasons for being here tonight, for doing what we can to aid in protecting the people of Geldania. We are all Sorcerers and seasoned warriors, just one of a dozen such groups fighting throughout the eastern lands.

Cheryl and Valla rose, gathered the bowls and spoons, and took them to the creek a short distance away.

Valla warned us of the intruders. <There are two people on the other side of the creek. If three of you can get behind them, the rest of us can come at them from the front, and we will have them caught in the middle. Perhaps you could help Midnight, considering you neglected to inform us of these two.>

Midnight snorted, <I am already here, watching our two guests, Valla. They are young and good at sneaking, and they are well armed. I will wait for you slow-pokes to catch up before I pounce.>

<Pam, Joanne, you're with me. Liam join Cheryl and Valla. Let us know when you're in place. Let's try to take them alive!> I knew the group would follow my directions without question.

<Midnight, where are you?> Cheryl asked.

<I am here looking at our visitors. They are two young girls, who seem to be no older than sixteen winters.>

<Everyone move in and be careful. We don't need anyone getting hurt tonight.>

As I motioned Pam and Joanne to follow me a commotion erupted in front of us.

"Get off me, you beast," one of the girls yelled. "Or I'll run you though with my sword!"

I produced a light as we approached the voice. Midnight's front paws were holding a distraught young red-haired girl down on the ground, and Cheryl had her arms around another young girl with reddish blond hair, keeping her from running or drawing the sword at her side.

"Both of you have the gift of sorcery, I see. You should know better than to try sneaking up on a camp full of Sorcerers," I said, trying to look stern. "Come on you two, you look like you haven't eaten in days. We have stew and bread and will see to it that you are fed before we send you on your way."

"We are hunting those filthy southerners, and we know you are too," said the one with reddish blond hair. "We have been following you for days now, let us join your company."

The Furl Cat let the other one up and Pam took her by the arm to lead her toward the camp.

Liam, ever the mediator, tried to break the tension. "I am Liam; you have met Pam, and Cheryl. This one is Joanne, that one is Valla, the Furl Cat is Midnight, and Richard is our leader. And you would be?"

The red-haired young lady looked around at those who had captured them.

"I am Tarisha and this is my sister Jakiera. The people who raised us called me Tara and my sister Jacky. We both grew up with a sword in our hands, and we have been well trained in their use."

"Jacky and Tara, it is then. You will have your meal," I told them, "and we will have a two-hour nap. When we awake, we will discuss whether you're coming with us or not."

The two young ones looked skeptical but didn't argue. After the meal I talked to Midnight and Scarlet before I lay down to sleep.

I looked at the two young ones. *I was not that much older than they are now when I started. We have been doing this for many winters, and we all wear the scars of those battles. A dozen names are etched into our minds: those we have buried, those who died fighting at our side. I see the same determination in Jacky and Tara as I see in my five cohorts. Do I have the right to deny them their chance at the revenge they look for?* I looked to the sky as I turned toward my bedroll, Borin, the smallest of the three moons, was high in the sky with Corin, the largest moon, just peeking over the horizon. There would be sufficient light for our journey south.

When we woke, I sought the others' opinions on whether Jacky and Tara should join us.

"I was still a child when you found me Richard. Those girls are sixteen winters old. I was fighting by your side when I was only ten winters. They are the same age as me now." Pam reminded me. "We will put it to a vote."

Although I was considered the leader, we followed a democratic approach in making decisions. The women had four votes to the men's two, so it was agreed that the two young ones would join the group.

"The two of you are part of our family now," I said. "We number eight, and that means that each of us could be facing odds of fifteen-to-one or higher. What we do is extremely dangerous. Do you understand what you have signed up for?"

"We understand and will do our best," Jacky said.

"Let us hope that will suffice," I replied.

With that taken care of, we packed our things for the journey south. I made it clear to the newcomers that there was no verbal chitchat while we traveled; they would talk telepathically. Midnight and Scarlet were our scouts, making sure the trail ahead was clear of any stray enemy soldiers.

Jacky asked Valla, "How do we talk with this telepathy?"

<I would rather they knew how before we arrive at our destination, Valla.>

Valla smiled. "Come with me and I will teach the two of you."

The road south would take us to the camp of the southern raiders only two hecna walking distance from where we were.

I listened in while Valla started teaching the girls how telepathy worked.

<I am talking to you in your minds, so we do not give our position away. That is why we talk this way.>

<This is your telepathy? Jacky and I have been talking like this since we were old enough to talk.>

<Well it seems the two of you already know how this works. I will show you how to talk to one, or all of us without letting our enemy hear you.> Valla said.

The small group walked at a quick pace and the two hecna passed quickly. Scarlet informed us all when the raiders were only a metronome away. I led the group to the edge of a meadow a short distance away and we waited for the Red Dragon to land. Jacky and Tara stood with mouths open, staring at the large red creature.

<Tara and Jacky, how good are you with your bows?> I asked.

<Jorden was a soldier. Him and the others that raised us made sure we knew how to use the weapons we carry. We are well trained and accurate,> Tara said.

<Excellent,> I said.

<Up you go. Scarlet will fly you above the raiders. The southern Sorcerers are dressed in black robes; you want to target them when you can. They will be in the center of their soldiers, hiding like the cowards they are. And try not to shoot Scarlet. An arrow though one of her wings might make your trip shorter than expected.>

The young ones were reluctant at first. They had seen dragons in the sky, but didn't know anything else about them, and they had never seen one this close.

<If you don't follow orders you will be left out and left behind on your own.> I pointed out.

They quickly agreed, but were still tentative as they mounted the Red Dragon. Scarlet used her powerful hind legs to launch herself, and her two charges into the night sky.

<You all know what to do,> I said to the rest of the group as we started out on the last metronome.

We had talked about using magic in these raids, but decided that because the soldiers did not use magic, using it against them would be wrong. The Sorcerers on the other hand used magic against us, so we had no problem returning the favor. We could see the glow from the fires through the trees as we approached the enemy camp. Liam began counting.

<There are at least 125 from my count. It is hard to tell how many, because there are to many already in their bed rolls. I might be off by twenty or more, either way,> he told me.

We split up, surrounding the camp. Scarlet was high enough not to be seen from below, but not so high that Tara and Jacky couldn't see their targets. The camp was silent; everyone seemed to be sleeping. When everyone was in position, I gave the word.

Arrows flew from around the camp making it appear they were being attacked by a large army. Every arrow found a mark. Two dozen arrows rained down on the unsuspecting camp within two heart beats. The first six of those had a fireball attached and struck the Sorcerers' tent. With the tent lit up, Tara and Jacky had no trouble finding the Sorcerers. I could hear the Sorcerers yelling to their soldiers, at the top of their lungs. "Kill them all!"

But it was not an organized defense; the soldiers fired their arrows, and the Sorcerers threw their fire and lightning, in every direction.

We released our arrows, changing positions constantly, moving around the camp, shooting arrows at will. This tactic gave the impression that there were more of us than there were. Unfortunately, we couldn't avoid all the danger coming our way. I caught an arrow in my thigh. I reached down and broke it off a centra from my leggings and kept moving, releasing arrow after arrow.

Joanne caught an arrow in the shoulder; she too broke it off so it didn't hinder her efforts. She kept moving as well, picking her targets on the run. But we were running low on arrows.

<Pull back! We need to regroup,> I said, my wound draining more than blood.

Pam, with Midnight's help, found me, while Valla found Joanne, and we all made our way back to the meadow a metronome away. Scarlet asked if anyone needed a lift, but she was assured we would manage.

Scarlet, Tara, and Jacky were waiting for us in the meadow when we arrived. Pam sat me down and worked on getting the arrow out of my thigh so she could mend the wound. Valla was taking care of Joanne's shoulder. Midnight patrolled the woods south of the meadow but doubted that we had been followed. Once the wounds were taken care of, we ate a cold meal and rested for a few hours, Scarlet and Midnight keeping watch.

---∘∘⊰◉⊱∘∘---

We discussed our next move, using thought so as to include those on watch. <How many soldiers do you think are left, Liam?> I asked. <Tara and Jacky, were you able to eliminate some of the Sorcerers?>

Liam scratched his chin. <You're asking a lot, Richard, but I would guess there's maybe eighty or ninety.>

Tara looked at me. <We did kill one of the six we saw before the fire died, and the others started using their soldiers as shields, making it harder for us to get at them, but we did manage to kill

two more, along with the soldiers protecting them, so there are three left.>

<We only have enough arrows left for one more raid, so we need to be prepared to go at them hand-to-hand. Are there any questions?>

No one had any questions, so we gathered our weapons and headed south one more time. I sent Jacky and Tara with Scarlet to be our eyes in the sky, and to eliminate the rest of the Sorcerers if they could get a shot at them. We were all short on arrows, but each of us gave the young ones an arrow to ensure they were able to eliminate the Sorcerers.

It was still dark when the enemy camp came into sight. When we arrived at the camp, Liam began counting heads. Most of the soldiers had returned to their bed rolls.

<Eighty-five give or take a few. It's hard to tell, they haven't removed their dead, and that's not counting the Sorcerers,> Liam said.

We attacked, using the same approach as before. But the soldiers were not sleeping and jumped up with bows in hand.

<They are giving us arrows, use them if you can,> I said. <That way we can even the odds a bit more.>

This time the southerners ran into the forest shooting arrows into the surrounding trees, probably trying to eliminate their enemy before we killed them. The Sorcerers threw lightning bolts and balls of fire with the same lack of accuracy as their soldiers shot their arrows. Our arrows were on target, narrowing the odds with every volley. All too soon our supply, even supplemented by southern arrows, ran out.

<It is time to meet them in hand-to-hand battle. Liam says there are only fifty or sixty soldiers left. How many Sorcerers are left, Tara?>

<There is only one, but he is surrounded by five of his soldiers. We need to kill the soldiers first and we are running out of arrows,> Tara answered.

<Get ready my friends,> I said.

We drew our swords. We came out of the woods from different directions, surprising the soldiers. Pam dispatched two, but was not quick enough to avoid the sword of a third. She suffered a gash to her right arm before removing his head. Pam, gritting her teeth, moved on, batting a sword away with her sword and stabbing with the other as she went.

Liam, a sword in either hand, seemed to be toying with two soldiers, countering one sword and then the other until he removed the sword arm of one, then the head of the other before turning back to the one-armed soldier and thrusting a sword into his chest. Liam struck down another attacker and side stepped one more, thrusting one of his swords up under the leather armor and into the heart of this new opponent.

The soldiers protecting the Sorcerers were shooting arrows at Jacky and Tara, and Scarlet had to keep maneuvering to avoid them, not for her own sake, but for the sake of her two charges. Scarlet was protected by her own built-in armor, while Tara and Jacky were not.

Joanne crouched down, ducking under a sword before she launched herself into the air, the sword in her left hand catching the soldier under his chin, as she drove it into his brain. She pulled that sword out as she pushed away from him with her left foot and she sailed over the head of another one, thrusting her sword into the back of his neck.

She pulled the sword out and landed on the shoulders of yet another soldier. With the sword in her right hand she decapitated the soldier to her right and thrust the sword in her left hand into the chest of the one she was standing on. She didn't notice the blood running down her left leg from the long gash from her hip to just above her knee.

I swung both swords: one at an attacker coming from the left and the other at one from the right. I placed my boot on the one to my right to free that sword. I sidestepped another and removed the hand of the soldier closest to me before sliding my other sword into his chest. I felt a sharp pain in my left arm and another in my right thigh. I never slowed my progress; I would take as many as I could before I dropped.

Four attackers surrounded Cheryl, but she moved with the agility of a Furl Cat. She was able to avoid most of the attackers' swords, but not all. A sharp pain in her side told her to turn, and she lashed out at the one who had caused her pain. She parried and thrust, turning and slashing. Cheryl turned, realizing that there were no more soldiers standing around her. She had eliminated all four of them, gritting her teeth, she moved on to her next target.

Valla danced around the soldiers, avoiding most of their attempts to stop her. She blocked a sword thrust and removed a head here and an arm there before drawing her sword across the one-armed soldier's neck.

Valla turned looking for her next target and stopped. Breathing heavily, we looked at one another as we realized that the battle was over. Now we had to take care of our injuries.

We walked to a clearing a short distance away. Each of us had injuries of some sort, and each one of us had torn strips of cloth off clothing to bandage wounds till they could be looked at.

Scarlet set herself down in the clearing and the young ones dismounted and joined us. Jacky and Tara went to Pam's side.

"How can we help? Show us what we need to do?"

It turned out that Jacky and Tara had no experience with healing, so Pam had them pay attention and showed both how to use magic to mend the damage inside the wound and how to close it when they were done. For the next couple of hours, they tended to the wounds of their new friends. Scarlet came back with a Kolten, already gutted and ready to butcher.

Once their wounds were taken care of Liam and Valla skinned and butchered the beast. The rest of us set up camp and had a large fire, complete with a grill made from green wood, waiting when Valla and Liam returned. Pam made bread dough from the rations found in the southerner's camp and formed it into loves.

"We will eat and rest before we begin the task of burying the dead," I explained to Jacky and Tara.

We worked together gathering the bodies and burying them. It took several hours. As before, we found that the soldiers only had the clothes on their backs, bed rolls, and weapons. The Sorcerers had jewelry and pouches of coins stashed in hidden pockets in their robes and cloaks—the ill-gotten spoils from those they had murdered as they terrorized villages and ranches on Geldanian soil.

We returned to the meadow a metronome away to collect the rest of our belongings and prepared another meal. It was quiet, as usually happened after the work was done: everyone trying not to think of the battle they had just fought. As much as we disliked our enemy, none of us liked taking another's life.

Today was over. For now, we would rest and recuperate from our injuries. When we were fully recovered, we would go in search of the next patrol of invaders.

---◦◦◦❯◉❮◦◦◦---

In his dreams, DeWayne saw Scarlet as a friend, but in many of the stories he had read, dragons were the villains who terrorized humans. He would like to see these dragons in real life.

CHAPTER 4

THE OTHERS

Midnight watched DeWayne as he continued writing. She knew where the others were but chose not to tell him until she was ready. Midnight had been exploring Canada for over five hundred years. She traveled coast to coast and from the US border to the North West Territories. During the last twenty years she had spent her time looking for people she deemed worthy of the gifts she carried. Midnight mused on her travels. She had spent the better part of twenty-five hundred years looking for a cure and a way home to no avail. She recalled her recent travels and the people she had met as DeWayne worked.

In the year 2034 she found a young man in the small town of Fergusons Cove, not far from Halifax, Nova Scotia. His name was Johnathan and he lived in a cottage overlooking the ocean. In the two months she stayed with him she learned who he was, what his past had been, and that he traveled around the world for his work. Johnathan was an only child. His mother, Mauna, was of African descent and his father, Johnathan, was Irish. They too were the only children born of their parents. Johnathan senior met Mauna in a military hospital where he was recovering from a gunshot wound he received in a confrontation with rebels who were trying to take over the government of Cameroon. When Johnathan senior recovered, they moved to Fergusons Cove, Canada.

Johnathan had dark brown curly hair and the dark skin of his mother and the Irish stubbornness of his father. He had blue green eyes and his six-foot-tall body was in good shape because of his work.

Johnathan looked at her and said he had to go back to work the next day, but he would ask his neighbor to look after her until he returned. She made her first choice and the night before she left she gave Johnathan the first gift: from Liam.

———◦∘◦}◎{◦∘◦———

Midnight already had people she had been keeping an eye on for several year as she moved from coast to coast and back again. Her next stop was North Bay in Ontario in the fall of 2035. She followed Bobby Joe home from the library where she worked. Midnight learned that Bobby Joe's mother, Sue Lin, was from Japan and her father, Jonas, was Norwegian. Sue Lin had been an instructor in martial arts and that is how she met Jonas. When they moved to North Bay, they opened a martial arts school together. Bobby Joe was raised learning the arts and practiced every day. She had no siblings, uncles, nor aunts left living, which made her the last of her family line. Her black hair, from her mother, had a few gray streaks and she had her mother's exotic Japanese features. She had her father's height, his blue eyes, and his stubborn demeanor. Midnight stayed with Bobby Joe for seven weeks and gave her the Sorcerer Cheryl's gift the night before she left.

———◦∘◦}◎{◦∘◦———

Midnight traveled to Sault Ste. Marie, making a few stops along the way because of the weather. It was the spring of 2036 when she found the twins Susan and Samantha. Midnight learned that they were both certified chefs and that they had lost their parents that past January. The twins were still trying to process the information the police had given them. It was a tragic tale to say the least. Brad and Alice had been stranded at an airport three hours away, according to the police investigation. They rented a car and were driving home in a blizzard when they were caught in a collision between a car and a semi-truck.

The twins were told their parents did not suffer, as death was instantaneous. Midnight was in a quandary because she could only give the gift to one of the twins and they had already suffered enough. She had a choice to make. *Do I separate these two by giving one of them the gift? Or do I move on and look for someone else?* She made her choice and decided to give the gift of the Sorcerer Joanne to Samantha. Midnight could only hope that Susan would be able to forgive her when she found out her sister would live a much longer life than she would.

————∞∘❦∘∞————

Midnight had met a couple in Thunder Bay thirty years before and decided to see if they still lived there. Philip and Bernice were good people and she wanted to look in on them. Midnight arrived in Thunder Bay in mid-July 2036 and found out that John and Bernice had been killed in a car accident by a drunk driver the previous year. But they had two children, twins, Adam and Amanda. Midnight chose to spend time with them to see if they had the same values as their parents had had.

She could see the pain they suffered from their loss, and learned that Adam was an accountant while Amanda managed a bar and bistro for an old friend of the family. Adam had an inoperable congenital heart defect; however, he could live a reasonably normal, although possibly shorter, life. Midnight took that into consideration when she inserted herself into their lives for a short time. Midnight decided that because of Adam's heart defect, Amanda was the better choice to receive the Sorcerer Pam's gift.

———◦◦◦⦗◉⦘◦◦◦———

Midnight's next stop was a long way off. She had met a couple of young doctors when she was in Vancouver almost forty years earlier. They had just graduated from university and they were madly in love. If they were still living there, she was sure she could find them and see how they were doing. They were both on her list of possible candidates for her second last gift. Midnight had already decided that DeWayne would get the final gift—if she could find him. He seemed to move around a lot.

Getting to Vancouver was a challenge, but Midnight arrived in the city in November 2036. She did not find the two she was looking for until the end of February 2037. Frank and Marie were much older, and they ran a lucrative practice. They took Midnight in and put an ad on the news asking if anyone was looking for a black cat. No one replied. Midnight spent two months with them and when she was ready to leave she gave Marie the Sorcerer Valla's gift. She was sure that Frank would understand.

———◦◦◦⦗◉⦘◦◦◦———

Now the search for DeWayne began. Midnight looked in the last place she had seen him and found that he had left years ago. In the summer of 2039 Midnight overheard a tourist speak of a man she knew who fit DeWayne's description. She followed this slim lead to Edmonton, Alberta.

It was the first week of September 2039 when Midnight found him entering a bar with his cart of groceries. The weather was changing. The days were getting shorter and the temperature was dropping below zero at night. In the past twenty years the weather patterns had changed drastically, Midnight feared winter would be upon them sooner than later.

She could sense him in the apartment building he lived in. Midnight gave him his longevity so she could sense his presence, read his thoughts. Everyone had a unique, invisible aura about them. Something that was visible to one with magic if they chose to look for it—a mental smell. The sun was setting, and it had started snowing big fluffy flakes again. She sensed he was agitated and when she read his mind, she knew he was leaving his apartment. She followed him to the bar and when he left, made sure he was going the direction she wanted him to go. DeWayne found Midnight, just as she planned.

Now she waited for him to ask the right question in the right way.

CHAPTER 5

SANCTUARY

It was the first week of November; the sun was going down when Midnight interrupted DeWayne's writing.

<I know your writing is something you need right now, but we have to take a trip!>

DeWayne looked up from his laptop. "Where are we going?"

<We need to go south and then west for a while, about a two-hour drive in all. We are going to an old hotel, and it is going to be our Sanctuary. I came across it in the late 1800s, when I was still looking for a cure for this disease. The place is large enough for everyone. It should be ready when the others come. You're going to need directions to put into your book, so they know how to get there.>

DeWayne frowned at her. "The others as in the others you gave the gift to?"

She looked at him, a confused look in her eyes. <Of course I mean the others with the gift. Who else is there? The gift isn't active in them yet; it's latent, but it will keep them healthy, and might improve them physically and mentally, but that would be all. Their gift still needs to be awakened before they can become Sorcerers.>

"Is this something that has to be done now, Midnight? I only have another day or two until I am finished writing this book."

<You are not listening to me. You're too busy with your nose stuck in that computer. You must include the directions to the Sanctuary in your book. So yes, this has to be done now.>

"Why do we need this Sanctuary, Midnight?"

<You are a Sorcerer now—with powers this world only dreams about. There are those that would take advantage of that given the chance. Governments around the world would seek you out and try and synthesize that power. Military would try and weaponize this gift to use it against their enemies. The general public would view you as a freak because they are afraid of what you can do. Exposing your gift to anyone will put your life in danger. There are five others who will come, and all of you must be protected from those that would do you harm.>

The surprise on DeWayne's face was obvious, but he agreed with her and began putting food, clothes, a couple of note pads, pencils, and his laptop computer into his backpack. Although he didn't need them anymore, DeWayne took his oakwood canes, too. He put on his Jason disguise as they left.

Once they were out of the city he changed back into DeWayne. He was thinking they must be close when Midnight told him to turn at the next road. It was blocked by snow, which faded as they approached. The car's headlights revealed a game trail. He turned and they were going west once more.

<This is the north road, and like the south road it is only visible to those with the gift. Both roads and the Sanctuary are hidden with magic.>

The winding road led them to a spacious clearing with a large two-story building at the back. As they drove up to the building DeWayne could read CONNORS WAY STATION in faded paint on the wide-plank siding. He stopped the car and a pint-sized tornado, or maybe it was a dust devil, sprang up moving from side to side, clearing the snow, opening a path to the stairs. He watched as it went up the steps to the building's door, turned and went along the balcony that seemed to wrap around the building.

DeWayne looked at Midnight. "You made a dust devil to clear the snow away?"

Midnight gave him her best smile as the dust devil disappeared around the corner. DeWayne turned the car off and a light appeared, lighting their way to the door.

Midnight's door opened and she jumped out. Jason, backpack in hand, followed her up the stairs.

He opened the door and Midnight went in first, producing three more globes of light, which spread out to illuminate the great room. He looked around as he closed the door, his breath visible in the cold air. There were two dozen tables with chairs in the spacious, open room. A line of pillars ran the length of the room. A fireplace in the middle of the room had a couple of couches and—what appeared to be—comfortable chairs surrounding it. Another fireplace stood against the wall to his right, with chairs and couches in front of it as well. It looked like the owners left in a hurry, taking only what they needed, or what they had room for in their wagons.

On one side of each fireplace was a large bin half-full of kindling and firewood. DeWayne built fires in both fireplaces. As heat began to seep into the room, he examined it in more detail. A bar stood along the west wall where glasses were neatly arranged on trays. Bottles of spirits sat on shelves in front of a mirrored wall. A stairway, in an alcove to the left of the bar, made a half turn around a pillar as it spiraled up to the next floor. There was a desk to the left of the stairs with a leather book lying closed on it. A peg board hung on the wall behind it with keys for the rooms. He opened the book to find that it was a record book for the rooms.

To the right of the stairs, between the stairs and the bar, was a rectangular wooden contraption that went from the ground floor through the second floor. DeWayne checked it to see what it was. There was a rope on his blind side that also went through the second floor. When he opened the door, he realized what it was: a dumb waiter for transferring luggage, food, and anything else that was too awkward to carry up the stairs. DeWayne made a mental note to modernize it when he figured out how he was going to do that. Beside the desk there was an opened door that led to a hallway going further into that part of the building.

DeWayne removed his backpack and set it on a table close to the central fireplace. Midnight jumped up on one of the comfy chairs and watched him.

<Are you going to look at the rest of the house, or get some food and rest?>

"Are you hungry, my friend? And yes, I am going to explore the rest of our Sanctuary right after we eat."

DeWayne collected the rest of their items from the car and made a quick meal. They ate in silence, DeWayne lost in thought about others taking advantage of them. Midnight was right. Keeping the Sorcery a secret was paramount.

Midnight lay down, wrapping her long tail around herself. DeWayne created a globe of light and went upstairs. At the top of the stairs a banister bordered the opening of the stairwell on two sides while the wall acted as the third one. The dumb waiter was built into the wall with an open section to access the rope pully. He counted three doors on either side of the hall before him and five on either side of the hall behind him, for a total of sixteen rooms.

He opened the first door and stepped in, letting his light reveal the interior. To his surprise it was larger than he had expected and fully furnished. Bed and dresser, writing desk and chair, couch and coffee table, and a table with a porcelain water jug and wash basin with a chamber pot tucked underneath. He should have expected that, though, considering that the downstairs was furnished. After checking two more identical rooms he assumed they were all the same.

As he went back downstairs, he let go of the light. He noticed the bottles behind the bar as he descended. Those that had been opened probably would not be palatable, but the ones that were still sealed should be okay. DeWayne made a note to check on that later.

The bar itself was well made, probably hardwood. It had a hinged section wide enough to walk through. As he walked through the opening DeWayne noticed swinging half-doors. Again, he brought up a globe of light and pushed through one of the doors into the kitchen. The light filled the large space revealing pots and pans hanging from hooks attached to the ceiling over a thick wooden table. Four wood-burning stoves stood against adjoining walls and, like everything else he had seen so far, they seemed to be well preserved. He would have to check items like this to ensure they still worked.

Two large sinks stood to the left of the two stoves on the west side, with a drying table next to them. There was a door beside the drying table that presumably led outside. He opened a door to his left and discovered it was a root cellar, stairs leading down to a large room with shelves for produce. As he walked back to the swinging half-doors, he noticed that one had a sign above it indicating it was the out-door. He had to chuckle at that. It seemed that common sense was alive back in the eighteen hundreds.

DeWayne went through the common room and walked into the hallway in the center of the east wall, his light moving before him above his head. He opened a door on his left; a sign above it said, *Clothing and Dry Goods*. Dresses and suits on hangers hung on wooden racks. Bales of cloth lay on shelving against one wall; barrels filled with flour, salt, sugar, and other dry goods were lined up in rows. Everything looked brand new, probably preserved by Midnight's magic.

On the other side of the hall another door led into an apartment of sorts. It went to the back of the building, with a window in the back wall. He stood in the dining room. There were three rooms separated with curtains. He stepped back out and closed the door. As he continued down the hall, the signs on the two remaining doors said *Hardware* and the last one was *Leather Goods and Tack Repair.* He checked the last door on the right and saw it was the same as the first room he had checked down the hall. The only difference was the furniture in here was of a much better quality, probably the owner's rooms. *I will make this my room when I am ready for bed,* he thought as he closed the door.

He returned to the common room. "It is as if we have been transported two hundred years back in time," he said to Midnight. "Everything is as it was two hundred years ago. I am impressed with your sanctuary Midnight. Most of this furniture is older than that and still well preserved."

<When I found this place, everyone had left. It was at the end of the gold rushes of that time, and the Klondike was just beginning. The road there bypassed the roads coming in here, so I imagine people quit using this road. It appears that they took only what they could fit in their wagons. I arrived here before looters could steal anything or cause damage to the place, as I have seen many times in my past. I put the magic shield up so no one else could find it again. The magic also preserved the contents. So, the open bottles of liquor, even as old as they are, will still be palatable.>

DeWayne prepared a decent meal for himself and Midnight over the open fire, choosing not to try and get the kitchen stoves working until the morning. He also tested one of the bottles of liquor before they settled for the night and slept for a few hours. DeWayne went down the hallway to the last room. He created lights that gave off enough heat to take the chill out of the air and looked around. Adding more stuffing to the bed with his magic was easy. Then he turned to the dresser. The mirror was faded—and was probably like that when it arrived—so he re-covered the back with a coat of silver oxide paint.

DeWayne looked at the old man reflected there, as if he were seeing himself for the first time.

What are you doing DeWayne? he thought.

Midnight was right, this you is dead and buried. The book you're writing is going to have Jason's picture on the back cover, not yours. If the others come, they will expect to see Jason—not you.

I think it is time you gave your head a good shake. Take advantage of the new you that you have created. It is not going to be easy, but when has anything ever been easy? YOU decided to let DeWayne go, then YOU changed your mind when your stubborn nature took over.

The image in the mirror changed. The old man became the younger virile persona of Jason. *This is DeWayne's new body so get used to it.*

Jason went to bed and slept.

⸺∘∘◦〉◉〈◦∘∘⸺

When he woke Jason walked into the common room, Midnight's ears stood up straight. <What is this I see? I thought you were going to remain your old self?>

"One can make a poor judgment and regret that choice. You were right my friend, this is who I chose to be when we started this, and now it is time for me to be who I should be, so let's move on."

After breakfast Jason went out the back door to explore the grounds and discovered the dust devil had cleaned around the house. At the back of the building, sitting in a niche on the balcony, was a metal monstrosity. He approached it and lifted the lid to find it was an outdoor grill, a barbeque, or a smoker. The inside was clean, and with the magic that protected this place there wasn't any rust or corrosion, nor any rodent nests that he could see. A glare caught his eye and he noticed a building of glass, probably a greenhouse, in the back yard.

He looked at the dusty panes of glass that made the roof, the glass on the walls was relatively clean. Inside were two levels of planters, twenty on each level on either side. A walkway down the center of the room allowed one to access those on the first level, and a stepladder at the back of the room could be used to access the upper level.

There was an open space, from the planters to the back wall, where a long wide table stood. He checked the earth in the planters and found it to be dry and hard. He frowned, taking in the view of the whole inside of the greenhouse. Why did it look so much larger inside than it did outside? He had to talk to Midnight about the discrepancy. Jason turned and left the greenhouse.

He could see another building through the trees. Making a small dust devil, he sent it a few feet ahead of him to clear the snow, making a path to a barn. He reached the barn door and let the small whirl wind dissipate before producing a light and entering the barn. There was a large open space before him. There was a blacksmith's forge with all the tools. The barn wasn't heated, but no doubt when the forge was in operation it would have been toasty in here. Beyond the forge were animal stalls. He left the barn and made his way back to the main building in search of Midnight.

"The greenhouse looks a lot bigger inside than it does outside. Would you by chance know anything about that?"

<The Sorcerers who were exiled with me from Orighen used to put up a small tent. On the outside, it looked like a normal tent, but on the inside, it was more than large enough for all of us. I learned a few things from my friends about using their magic but had no need to try this one until I found this place. I chose the greenhouse to try it out. I suppose you would like to know how?>

Jason looked at her, confusion written on his face. Midnight jumped up beside him and touched his cheek with her paw. He saw how she did this little bit of magic. He practiced giving his backpack twice the room it normally had; after two or three dozen tries, he finally had it figured out. It worked even better than he expected.

Jason looked at the black cat. "So, I can use this on anything I want to make bigger on the inside?"

<I have given you the knowledge, but it is up to you to figure out what you can, or cannot, do with it. I believe there is a variation that can also makes things bigger and smaller; however, you will have to experiment and find out for yourself what works.>

"Ok, before I go back to my writing, I will make some notes of the changes I need to make, what materials I need, what I can do without materials. If making changes is all right with you, my friend."

Midnight snorted, closed her eyes, and went to sleep.

Jason started his list with modern conveniences such as plumbing for the Sanctuary itself, and a small source of electricity—either a generator or solar panels—for a fridge and to charge electronic devices. He would have to figure out how he was going to bring water into the greenhouse and the main building, maybe the barn too. He should also make sure the rooms upstairs were comfortable. Then he sat at the table thinking. Midnight said he had to have an address or location to put in his book. He opened his laptop and discovered that there was no internet signal at the Sanctuary, so he added a note to find something so he could use to access the internet.

CHAPTER 6

RENOVATION

<J ason you have been at that for hours. You should put your book aside for now, and concentrate on the here and now.>

Jason looked at Midnight. "The book needs to be finished if we are going to let the others know how to get here!"

<Yes. I understand that, but this place also needs to be habitable when they arrive.>

The new year—a new decade—2040, was only a week old, but Midnight was correct. Jason reviewed the list of materials he needed and could not think of anything else. They made the trip to Edmonton and Jason made his purchases over the following week, expanding the car's carrying capacity as needed. He finished the first draft of the book, except for adding the GPS co-ordinates.

When they returned to the Sanctuary, his first project was to attach a satellite dish to the roof and run wiring to a main router in the common room. Midnight showed him how to use his magic to move something from one place to another and how he could levitate himself as well. Levitating his own body took more energy than moving an inanimate object, for some reason Midnight could not explain or didn't think it was necessary to explain. With the new internet connection, it was easy to obtain the GPS location of the building. In between projects Jason went for walks, exploring the property he would call home. That is how he found the stream.

His next project was getting water from the stream running through the property to the barn, the greenhouse, and main house. First he built a pump house by the stream and used magic to heat it. All the water lines that were outside he protected from freezing with magic as well. Every room in the house that needed water got it, although he still needed sinks, bathtubs, and toilets.

The greenhouse had a sufficient heating system, and a watering system that would give a trickle of water to all the plants. Jason rejuvenated the soil that was already there with the nutrients needed for growing healthy plants and produce. He would plant seeds for a variety of edible plants once he found the seeds he would need. Finally, he retrofitted the dumb waiter with an electric motor to run it up and down, with buttons upstairs and down.

With that all done, they went back to the city so he could work on getting his novel published. According to Midnight all the others lived somewhere in Canada. Jason remembered how long the publishing process had taken for his previous books and he did not think there would be enough time. Midnight was always in a rush to get everything done.

Jason sat down beside Midnight. "How can you be so sure that everyone you gave the gift to, will read my novel? I don't have your level of certainty that they will."

<I lived with each of the others long enough to know their habits. All of them like to read fantasy fiction. Like you, they all believe deep down that Earth is not the only planet that has sentient beings. Writing that last page in the language of Orighen will also get their attention.>

"Yes, the language of Orighen is very similar to the rune language of the ancient Norse. I am sure that no one is going to question my use of it," Jason agreed.

Jason considered what Midnight told him. "There must be a better way to reach them. Can we use telepathy? Would that not be easier than taking a chance that they will all find and read my novel?"

<You put your faith in knowledge you acquired from reading science fiction and fantasy novels. I will try and explain the realities. Yes, we can talk to each other here, and even a short distance away from each other. The others live hundreds, thousands of kilometers away from here. Even if you could transmit your thoughts that far, it would not work. You need to know the person you're talking to, and know exactly where they are. Looking for alternatives is a good thing, but you have to trust me! Write the co-ordinates to the Sanctuary somewhere in your book. I have time left if I am careful. >

"You are always telling me your time is running out, and this book thing you seem to be fixated on is going to take time. The book itself is finished. I can edit it, and, if I need to, I can publish it myself. All of that is still going to take months. Do we have that kind of time to do this your way?"

<Time to me is not the same as time is for you. I have been on this world for three thousand years, and Furl Cats existed for ten thousand years before I was sent here. Twenty, even a hundred, years is a short time for me. I am weaker now than I was twenty years ago, and my ability to use my magic has diminished considerably. The magic I am using to teach you is minimal compared to what I was once capable of using. I have the same virus that killed the Sorcerers. I believe that taking their magic into me is the reason I am still here today. Now that I have given the magic to the six of you, the virus is beginning to take its toll. If I preserve the magic I have left, I will last longer; therefore, my use of magic is limited to helping you understand the magic I have given you. You, on the other hand, are not limited in how much magic you use.>

Jason still looked skeptical.

<I can see you're still not convinced. The others will be having similar dreams to the ones you have. When they see the cover,

they will look at the book; the title will capture their attention. When they get to the last page, they will understand what they read because the gift, even though it isn't awake in them, will help them understand. You need to trust me on this.>

Jason shook his head and did a search online for self-publishing. He found articles and sites that offered to help you with the process for a fee. True Style Publishing offered cover design, editing, marketing, and distribution—and about a six-month turn-around. A quick check of the Better Business Bureau showed them to be a legitimate company.

"It would help if I knew where these people lived Midnight."

<I can tell you which city each of them lived in at the time I gave them the gift, if you think that might help. I cannot guarantee they are still living there though. However, they all had good jobs and owned their own homes, so I doubt they have left that behind.>

Jason was incredulous. "You knew all this time? I have mentioned that knowing where the others are located would be beneficial, yet you have not said anything until now. If they were comfortable where they lived when you found them, then the chances are good that they are still there."

Jason could sense when Midnight was smiling, and what he sensed right now was not pleasant.

<If you ask the right question you will get the answer you need. I know you are not pleased with the way I do what I do, but trust me, I have my reasons.>

"Give me the names of the cities and I will forgive you for waiting until now to share this with me." Jason smiled to ease the reprimand in his voice. "I will add the directions somewhere on the cover, so it is in plain sight."

At the end of February Jason sent an email to True Style asking them for a full list of alternatives within his budget. He knew he wanted an edit on the manuscript, and would probably have to make changes, but he already had cover art sketched—perfecting it, however, would be up to their designer. He received an answer that afternoon and after careful consideration he decided this was the way to go. He sent everything they asked for—manuscript, cover art, title page, and table of contents—with his payment; now the rest was up to them.

Jason went to the hardware store. He purchased a few things, but he was there to look at bathtubs, sinks, faucets, and fridges so he could use magic to replicate them.

—∘∘◦]◉[◦∘∘—

Midnight and Jason returned to the Sanctuary. They fell into a comfortable routine as Midnight used the work modernizing their home as teachable moments. There were occasional emails from True Style as the cover art was tweaked, which Jason liked.

Jason lengthened the growing area of the greenhouse using the magic trick Midnight taught him for making things larger inside. He planted fruit trees and other plants that needed room to grow, such as potatoes and various types of squash, in these beds. He wanted the Sanctuary to be self-sufficient.

"What do you think about getting some chickens, turkeys, pigs, and cows?" Jason asked Midnight once the planting was done.

<You can use magic to make all of that, so I see no need for them.>

"They would be there for teaching purposes only. I could get laying hens and a couple of milk cows; that way there would be milk and eggs. When the others come, what better way is there to teach them than using the real thing?"

Finding a truck and trailer to haul the livestock and fowl proved to be easier than he had anticipated. Now he needed to make the barn their home.

First, he enlarged the space at the back of the barn so the cows would have plenty of room to graze. Jason gave the pigs more room as well. He added a trough for feeding, a mud hole for them to cool off in, and a lean-to lined with straw for them to sleep. The chickens and turkeys had a pen together. The chickens had coops lined with hay to sleep in and lay their eggs. The turkeys had a place they could go to when they wanted to sleep as well.

When he was done with living quarters for the livestock, he stood in the open space at the front of the barn trying to figure out how he was going to heat it. As he looked around the large space, he could see the possibility for an exercise room. He would look at different equipment the next time he was in the city. As for heating he would use magic, the same as he had in the main building and the greenhouse. Of course, he could always use the forge for heating in the coldest months.

In his dreams, the Sorcerers on Orighen used swords, knives, and bows and arrows, as their weapons—many infused with magic—to do battle with their enemies. Jason researched the best metals to forge knives, swords, and arrowheads. He also researched the best woods for making bows and arrows. Some of the wood used by professionals could be found right there on the Sanctuary grounds, but he would have to obtain the metals he needed.

His research gave him blueprints showing dimensions and weights for a variety of blades and weapons. He had been one of five certified blacksmiths in the province forty years ago, so he possessed the knowledge to work the forge and make what he needed. DeWayne's lifetime of work as a fabricator and welder had its advantages. He saved all the documents he had found regarding the weapons he planned on making for reference.

Jason, with list in hand, made a trip into the city. He found all the materials he was looking for, then he made his purchase of two milking cows—a cow was still a cow regardless of what its intended use was—and other animals.

With the truck and trailer both loaded to the brim with livestock and material, he made his way back to the Sanctuary.

The cows, pigs, turkeys, and two dozen laying hens seemed to like their new residence.

The open area in the front of the barn he filled with different exercise equipment. The side wall had hooks and brackets, ready for the weapons he would be making. Overhead were globes of light that turned on with motion, and off when there was no activity for a short period of time. Almost everything was produced with magic, as was most of the heat.

———◦◦○❉○◦◦———

In one of the dreams Jason had had, he watched an elven blacksmith as he made two swords for Richard, infusing them with magic as he worked. That seemed a good place to start. It was slow going at first because it had been the better part of forty years since he had practiced blacksmithing. At least he could use telekinesis to move large items to where he needed them. He found coal for the forge in an abandon coal mine not far from the Sanctuary and had access to plenty of dead trees in the forest surrounding them for igniting the coal. He worked at the forge after his regular daily chores were completed.

Jason made molds from clay for the handles that would be used for the swords and knives, shaping each one to the designs he had created from the dream-memories. The hilt was part of the sword and took time to make depending on how elaborate the design was. He hammered the steel out, infusing it with magic each time he folded the steel over, making it stronger and more resistant to nicks and breaking. When he was finished the first sword, he held the hilt with both hands, closed his eyes, and went through the motions from his dreams. The sword was heavy but not overly so, yet when he was finished the moves, he was feeling muscles he didn't know he had. *This will be a fine way to exercise.*

Something else he remembered was the staff that Richard carried. He took his canes and merged them together using magic.

When he was finished, the staff was as long as he was tall. The handles of the canes formed the top of the staff making it larger at the top than the bottom. It would be another weapon infused with magic in his arsenal.

On the first day milking the cows Jason realized he was going to have more milk than he could use. Cows had to be milked twice a day. He cleared his mind and thought of what else milk could be used for. Butter was made from milk and so was cheese. Jason went online and looked for machines for making butter and cheese from the 1800s. To his surprise the items he needed were identical to items in the kitchen closet, which he hadn't been able to identify. He saved the blueprints for both, in case he ever had to repair them, and instructions on how to use them to make cheese and butter.

It had been six weeks since he'd had any word from True Style and Jason was starting to doubt his choice of self-publishing using a contractor when he received an email from them. It contained a letter stating the changes they believed he should make and their reasons for said changes, along with a copy of the manuscript with those changes highlighted. The changes they wanted to make were minor. Jason had an advantage over other writers—as a Sorcerer his ability to find mistakes in the manuscript was more accurate than most. He accepted the changes and sent it back. His first novel had taken almost two months before the editing was done. Publishing it took several more months. He hoped this would be faster.

It was another two months before Jason heard back from True Style that his book would be printed, and the marketing was already happening. They said they would contact the bookstores in the cities he had asked them to, but that it would be up to those stores to choose whether they would sell his book. Another two months went by before True Style contacted him to say the stores he chose had accepted his book, and most of the stores they had chosen would sell it too. It was also being sold online. Jason received a higher payment than expected about six weeks later.

Now all they could do was wait and see if Midnight's predictions would hold true.

CHAPTER 7

FROM A DREAM: PART 2

Through all this the dreams hadn't stopped,
and Jason continued to document them.

The Invasion of Geldania

I watched as Cheryl and Pam sparred with Jacky and Tara. In the three heclona since the two had wandered into camp they had learned much from the company. We learned a few things from them in return. They had passed through settlements, large and small, in their travels, and Jacky was good at talking with the people they met. She had a diplomatic air about her. People listened to her, where my gruff tone and demeanor usually turned people away. Tara was interested in learning the strategical part of what we did, and she had potential.

Liam and I leaned up against a Lima tree. Its trunk was made from three smaller trees that wound around each other and presented a large umbrella like canopy. "Do you want half of this melon or not? You keep looking at that girl and she is going to catch on that you like her." Liam said as he offered me half of the Lima Melon.

"What are you talking about? I am just thinking is all." I blushed as I took the offered melon.

It was late in the day when Scarlet informed us that there was a farmhouse about three hecna ahead of the southern raiders, just off the road they were following.

I spoke with the others. "We have to send someone ahead to warn them that the southern soldiers and Sorcerers will be there soon." <Scarlet, would you take whoever volunteers to the farmhouse?>

"I'll go," said Jacky.

Scarlet landed on the road a short distance ahead and Jacky scrambled up to her back.

"Jacky, if they are willing to fight, let Scarlet know. If not, then make sure they are someplace safe," I instructed her.

"We should get ahead of the southerners and do as much damage as we can to slow them down. They should be stopping in another hecna or two to set up camp for the night, but they may not, they don't have a dragon in the sky watching over them or scouting ahead of them, as we do," Valla said.

We agreed and increased our pace. When we could see the dust from the marching southern soldiers we faded into the forest on either side of the road.

<We will follow them for a hecna or until they stop for the night, if they don't stop, then we will attack,> I said.

Not long after we had gained on the soldiers, they came to a field on the righthand side of the road. There were half a dozen Kolten grazing in a corner of the field. The southern Sorcerers decided to make camp, and they had meat for food right there. With over a hundred and fifty soldiers and six Sorcerers the field wasn't big enough for the southerners and the Kolten. I watched as one of the Sorcerers ordered a dozen archers to go with him. They skirted the tree line until they were close enough to attack the large creatures lying on the grass and killed one. The rest of the herd ran off looking for a safer haven.

The Sorcerer yelled at the soldiers to hurry. The soldiers gutted the animal, then butchered it. Another dozen soldiers, ran into the field to help carry the meat back to the camp. With the amount of meat they left behind I sent Valla and Liam to where the Kolten's carcass was. They stayed out of sight until the Sorcerer led the soldiers back to their camp then preserved what was left of the meat for later.

<We will find a place to rest until nightfall. We can make plans for our attack then,> I suggested.

We moved through the forest like a light breeze through the trees until we came upon a small clearing. Midnight stood guard. The southern Sorcerers were not concerned about guards or scouts—didn't seem to feel the need for such precautions. We settled on the ground and ate cold leftovers from the midday meal.

Scarlet and Jacky returned soon after we arrived at the clearing. Jacky explained what happened during her visit with farmer Bram and his family. <They are safe, and when I go back, I should have no trouble finding them—with Scarlet's help that is.>

Jacky took out her own leftovers. <I told them there were over one hundred and fifty soldiers coming their way and that they did not have the manpower to fight them. Then I asked, 'Do you have a safe place for everyone?'

<Bram said, 'We have a place a couple of metronomes north of here.' And he told his mate, Zada, to take the girls and gather provisions for a few days. Bram told Glen, his lead field hand to bring the hands in. 'How will we know when the danger has passed or eliminated?' He asked me.>

<I told him I will go back and find him with news whatever happens tonight. They will be safe Richard.>

As the sun was going down, we stretched our muscles preparing for the night ahead.

<We have at least six Sorcerers and about one hundred and fifty soldiers.> I knew I was repeating what they already knew, but

it had become a standard part of every raid. <You all know what to do. Grab your gear and let's get this done.>

We moved out in single file through the trees. Jacky and Tara sat on Scarlet's back waiting for nightfall. The sisters would be our eyes in the sky, and they would also take out as many of the southern Sorcerers as they could.

The invaders' camp was quiet. There was only one tent in the camp, and we knew that is where the Sorcerers would be. <Surround the camp and concentrate on the tent first, then we will deal with the soldiers.>

Six flaming arrows lit the night sky as they raced toward the black tent. Two more flaming arrows came from the sky, and the tent burst into flames.

Five of the six Sorcerers ran from the blazing tent trying to shed their burning robes. The soldiers jumped from their blankets, some pulling swords from sheaths, others stringing bows and slinging quivers over their shoulders. One of the Sorcerers went down with an arrow in his chest. The other four, now free of their robes, began throwing balls of fire and bolts of lightning in every direction.

Soldiers with bows circled the four remaining Sorcerers. They were protecting their masters from enemy arrows. We had done this dozens of times, each of us moving around the camp and we kept using this tactic because it confused both Sorcerers and soldiers, making them think they were being attacked by an army. We concentrated on the outer line of soldiers, who were shooting their arrows randomly into the forest trying to pick us off.

I saw some soldiers run into the forest, swords drawn. <Fall back, we do not want to fight them hand-to-hand yet.> Only fifty of the soldiers had fallen.

We returned to the clearing three metronomes from the battle site. Several of us had minor wounds. Valla and Liam came into the clearing with two large pieces of meat for our meal. I saw Scarlet land, folding her wings as the sisters jumped to the ground.

"Can you two please tend to the wounded," I asked them.

Pam, Cheryl, Joanne, and I had lacerations where arrows had grazed us. Stopping the bleeding and applying bandages was all Jacky and Tara could do for now. The wind was coming from the northwest, so building a cook fire was not a problem. I sat and watched as Valla and Liam put the meat on the grating Liam had made from green wood. After our wounds were tended to, we ate our hot meal and rested. Unlike the southerners I did post a guard. Midnight, took that duty. When we woke, I told them to prepare for the next attack.

———∘∘❀∘∘———

There was no time to replenish quivers before we attacked again, but it had become standard practice to use the enemy's arrows if we could. Bow strings were checked for wear, swords, and knives for nicks. Two hours later we were ready. <It's time to go,> I said. <Tara, Jacky, you're with Scarlet. We have one more battle left to fight.>

The smallest of the three moons was up, but we didn't need much light. Our night vision was enhanced by magic, magic we were born with. We surrounded the camp as we had before. The southern Sorcerers tent was surrounded by their soldiers as if they were waiting for us.

<Jacky, Tara, you have a better chance of eliminating the Sorcerers from up there. The rest of us will deal with the soldiers,> I said.

The battle began. The soldiers were up much faster than I expected they would be, and those were not Sorcerers sleeping in the tent. The first volley of arrows from our bows was met with arrows, balls of fire, and lightning bolts. The Sorcerers were mixed in with the soldiers, dressed in the same clothing and armor as the soldiers—except for the five soldiers dressed as Sorcerers in the middle—so it made it that much harder to pick them out of the crowd.

Jacky and Tara communicated that they could see the Sorcerers throwing their fire balls and lightning, so they were concentrating on picking them off one by one. More soldiers were dropping with every volley, but our arrows were running out even with the arrows we snatched up on the move.

The last Sorcerer began throwing ball after ball of fire at random, imagined, targets.

<We don't have a clear shot,> Jacky said. <He's surrounded himself with half a dozen soldiers.>

<But we have ten arrows left between us, and seven targets,> Tara said. <We will have to eliminate the lot.>

I could sense that they were amazed at the complete disregard the Sorcerers had for their followers, willing to sacrifice their men to preserve themselves.

Soldiers moved into the forest that surrounded the clearing. The rest of the soldiers continued to fire arrows into that same forest, not caring if they killed one of their own.

<We need to dispatch the ones coming after us,> I said. <Then we can come at them, hand-to-hand, from three different directions. Jacky, Tara, do what you can to get at that last Sorcerer.>

The soldiers entering the forest had their swords drawn and were ready for battle. The only sound was that of the soldiers walking through the trees, and the sound of their comrades' bow strings being released. I was near enough to see Cheryl watching a soldier walk past where she was concealed behind a tree. He was looking left and right. He would never make a tracker with all the noise he was making. She brandished one of her knives and grabbing him under the chin from behind, she sliced his throat, laying him onto the moss-covered ground.

<One down, I'm coming to you Pam.> We used an 'open' style of communication during battle, so we could all hear each other.

Our magic enhanced our night vision far beyond that of our attackers. Pam saw the soldier approaching, and before he knew what hit him, his head lay a couple of metra away.

<Two down,> Pam said.

Liam moved toward another soldier. The moonlight, peeking through the forest canopy, sprinkled small pools of light, and left everything else in dark shadows. Liam stopped in one of these shadows and waited. When the soldier walked into that same shadow, Liam struck.

<Three down. I am coming to you, Joanne.>

With all the soldiers who had entered the forest eliminated, Valla and I took a position east of the field where the last of the soldiers still shot arrows into the forest.

<Is everyone ready?>

Cheryl and Pam chimed in that they were ready. Liam and Joanne did so as well.

<How are things going up there Tara?> I inquired.

<They are getting low on arrows,> said Tara. <However, we still have a few left, so it shouldn't be long now. You're good to go. This one is more interested in us.>

Liam and Joanne moved into the open from the south, with Liam in the lead and Joanne a few feet behind and to his left. Liam battled those ahead and Joanne battled those coming in from behind.

Pam and Cheryl moved in together from the west, until they were upon the surprised soldiers; Pam charged ahead while Cheryl covered her back. Then Pam fell back and Cheryl led the charge while Pam covered her back.

Valla and I, back to back slowly turned as we moved in from the east, protecting each other, and fending of any attacks from all sides. As Valla turned, she came face to face with Cheryl, swords ready for action. Valla lowered her swords when she realized who was in front of her.

We looked around and realized that the battle was over.

Jacky and Tara released their bowstrings and the last soldier fell. Their last two arrows found the last Sorcerer's heart.

The battle was over.

Scarlet circled the field before she landed a short distance away. We treated our wounds first. Then while Valla and Liam built a travois large enough to carry the carcass of the Kolten—we would smoke-cure the meat we didn't use for our meal, preserving the rest of it for later use—the rest of us began digging a grave large enough for the southerners.

"Gather all the arrows," I said once that was complete. "We can use the unbroken ones for our next battle and salvage the arrowheads. Collect anything else that might be useful." It wasn't as if they needed my direction, but we had learned that these reminders ensured everything got done when we were all tired.

As she finished her tasks Tara asked, "Why are there no Geldanian soldiers around? We have been fighting these southern raiding parties for years and haven't seen one sign of King Arin's army."

"Perhaps for now you should ask Scarlet if she would take you and your sister back to the farmer and tell them it is safe to return home." I said. We needed to heal, rest, and regain our strength. We could worry about the lack of soldiers, and decide our next move tomorrow.

When Scarlet found the farmer Bram's safe haven she landed in an open area. "The threat has been eliminated" Jacky told Bram. There is no longer danger to your people. You can return home now." Bram and his family expressed their thanks and Jacky jumped onto Scarlets back behind her sister.

As they flew back to the others Tara told Jacky that someone had to find out why the king's army was not there helping with this southern scourge. The two of them agreed that they would go to Geldan and talk to the king.

I watched as Tara and Jacky stalked toward us the moment they dismounted from Scarlet on their return.

"We have decided to go to Geldan, our capital city, and talk to the king. We will return with Geldanian soldiers as soon as we can." Jacky told us.

I looked at her and Tara. "The two of you have come a long way since we first found you. I have no doubt that you can make the trip to the capital, but it will be dangerous."

The next morning, at dawn, I watched as Jacky and Tara prepared to leave. I wanted to say something to Jacky but thought that would be inappropriate. She was only ten winters younger than I was, but I had my part to do and she hers.

CHAPTER 8

BECOMING A QUEEN

As Jacky secured her bedroll to her backpack she glanced at Richard and blushed—he was looking at her again. When she looked at him emotions she had never felt before welled up inside her. Once you got past the gruffness of him, he was easy to talk to. She was going to miss him most of all.

Tara and Jacky passed through a couple of villages on the first day of their journey. Jacky talked to people on the streets and in the inns asking questions about Geldanian soldiers. The responses were not promising. As the day was waning, they approached another town.

"We can stay at an inn tonight," Tara said. "It will be nice to have a bed to sleep in for a change."

Two women and two men walked out of the trees ahead of them and approached the sisters. Tara drew one of her swords.

"We are prepared to defend ourselves if you intend to rob us."

The four strangers stopped. One of the women stepped forward. "We mean you no harm. Do you not recognize us? We talked at the Inn in Danby earlier today."

Jacky looked at the four and frowned. "You are following us? Why?"

"You said you fought with a group of rebels whose leader is called Richard. We have heard of him and the people who fight with him. We too are Sorcerers who fight the invaders from the south. I did not fully answer your questions because we had to be sure you are who you say you are. I am Bella and these are my friends Cecil, Bart, and Gigi. Come with us and we will tell you what we are doing that coincides with your quest. We have a camp set up a metronome to the west of the town."

Jacky looked at Tara, who was still holding her sword in a menacing way. "Put that away Tara you won't be needing it." She turned to Bella. "I believe what you say, take us to your camp and tell us what you can on our way there."

"No real bed again tonight," Tara said as she sheathed her sword.

As they walked Bella told them that a few heclona ago she had had the same thought as Jacky and decided to do something about it. She told the sisters that she had met dozens of Geldanian soldiers who had been released from service and sent home by King Arin ten winters ago. The notice from the king only stated that Geldania was not in any danger and that an army was no longer needed. One sergeant had said the soldiers had not seen the king for several winters prior to that announcement. That sergeant was gathering as many soldiers as he could find to go to Geldan and confront King Arin—if the king was even alive.

As they traveled they met more Sorcerers who wanted answers as well. When they arrived at the camp they were fed a hot meal, then they were assigned to a small tent. To Tara's surprise it had several comfortable looking cots. "I guess I spoke too soon, those look much more comfortable than sleeping on the ground."

The next morning they were summoned to a meeting in a large tent. Several high ranking Geldanian soldiers were present, all wearing their uniforms. A tall silver-haired soldier stood in front of those gathered. "I will make this short, as I know that many of you have traveled far to get here. There are two more camps north-east of Geldan that hold over a thousand soldiers and dozens of Sorcerers. We break camp in the early morning tomorrow and begin our journey west. To avoid any suspicion, we will travel in groups of no more than ten and we will leave at half hecna intervals. Travel will also be faster than going in a large group. If there are any questions, ask them now." No one spoke. "Thank you all for joining our cause, I will see you in the morning."

Tara and Jacky joined Bella's company of seven Sorcerers. Jacky woke before dawn, called Tara, and they gathered their belongings. The journey to the next camp took two-and-a-half heclana. The camp was well organized, with the tents, most of them large enough to hold a dozen soldiers, neatly erected in rows. Bella led them to a large tent where soldiers in uniform stood around a table covered in maps.

"Good morning, Sirs. We have come from the east to join in the fight. Can one of your men show us where to pitch our tents?"

The soldier that led them to the camp, the one with the silver hair, spoke to the man standing beside him and came over to Bella. "I am General Holten and I will get you settled in. And you are?"

"I am Bella and I come with nine of my friends."

The old man smiled as they stepped outside. "Come along you lot, we have tents that are not being used and more being set up every day."

The general walked beside Bella asking her questions about where they came from. Bella told him about others who should be arriving throughout the day. He assured her they would be welcome. Over the next heclana they all helped with camp work: making bows and arrows, and preparing food for the growing number of soldiers and Sorcerers.

On the seventh heclena General Holten sent for them. "I have summoned you here to ask you to lead a strike force into the palace. Six aqueducts run under the city taking waste to the ocean. One of these will take you into the palace. All of you have been active in our fight against the invaders and I believe you are our best choice. Bella, you spent several years in the palace, so you know the layout better than most. The way in is not an easy one; however, it can be done with the right people—and I believe you are our best choice. Will you volunteer to take this task on?"

Bella looked at Holten. "Can we discuss this among ourselves before we commit to your plan, Sir?"

"You have one hecna Lady Bella, we must begin our assault today."

Bella asked her cohorts if they were up to the incursion into the palace. The decision was unanimous. One hundred soldiers, led by Commander Doren, were also in the party. They looked at maps and diagrams that showed where the underground aqueducts were and how to access them from above and came up with a plan. The company rappelled down the slope to the discharge end of the aqueduct. Once inside they found walkways on either side of the channel and lights on one side made it easier to navigate than expected.

Commander Doren walked beside Bella and finalized the details of their raid. "We do not know what we will find in there. If our suspicions are correct, we may be looking at a battle that some of us will not come back from. A two-pronged attack—you take fifty soldiers and I take the rest."

"We know the risks involved Commander. Can you and your men use telepathy to communicate?" Bella asked him.

"Some of us can. I suppose shouting would not be to our benefit would it?"

Bella took Tara, Jacky, Cecil, and Bart with her while the other four Sorcerers went with Commander Doren. They reached the points where they would ascend into the palace. Bella gave the word and both parties climbed the stairs. Bella come out in the kitchen. One of the soldiers moved ahead checking for kitchen staff, but no one was there. *So far so good,* Bella thought. There was a service stairway in the kitchen that would take them to every floor of the palace. They climbed the stairs to the floor that housed the king's private rooms. That is when everything went south.

A dozen soldiers guarded King Arin's chambers and the first battle began. The soldiers guarding the hallway were not Geldanian, they were from the southern continent. The fight in the hall was short, but they had more soldiers and two southern Sorcerers to deal with once they entered the main room. Jacky fought her way to the king's bed chamber and, throwing her knife at the Sorcerer guarding the door, was able to gain access to the room.

She found an old man lying in the bed, he was alive but just barely. At a sound behind her she turned in time to swing her sword at the soldier charging toward her. More soldiers came through the doors, and the battle lasted for several hecna before they defeated the last of the southern attackers. Jacky could hear the clang of swords in the hallway and prepared herself for more fighting. Bella, Tara, and Cecil came into the room. Tara and Cecil stood by the door watching for any trouble.

Bella approached the bed. "Is he alive?"

"He is Bella, but he needs a healer sooner than later."

"Do you hear that?" Tara said.

Bella and Jacky turned. "Silence, it sounds as if the fighting has stopped."

Healers were brought in to see to King Arin's maladies. Ten heclena passed and Jacky spent as much time as she could watching over the king.

Jacky was sitting by Arin's bed when he woke and looked at her. "Who are you?"

"I am Jakiera, King Arin, but my friends call me Jacky. The palace was taken over by southern Sorcerers and their soldiers. It took us some time before we realized that something was amiss here in the palace. We have secured the city and there are patrols searching for stragglers. I took it upon myself to recall the soldiers and sent over a thousand east to deal with the raiding parties our resistance fighters have been dealing with for the past decade. I will bring one of the healers in."

"Do not leave me young lady, I like your company."

She summoned a healer from the next room and the healer told Jacky that King Arin would not see the end of this heclona. He has been tortured and there was no way of undoing the damage done. Jacky sat by the king as he slept.

"I spoke with Bella this morning." King Arin said when he woke from one of his naps, "She tells me you have been taking care of the business end of running the palace and the city. I heard the healers talking and know that my time is almost up. Geldania needs a ruler. From what I am being told you sound like the perfect choice for that position."

Jacky was surprised at the enthusiasm in his voice. "I am not the person for such an important position my King. I am an orphan warrior. Where is your family, I heard you had children?"

"I am told that the southern Sorcerers murdered my family, so there is no one else. You are a Sorcerer; you are a beautiful woman and I want to make you my mate before I pass, take my hand and become my Queen. I am the one who chooses my successor. There is not much time left to me, so I would ask you not to think too long on my request."

Jacky talked the king's request over with Tara and Bella.

Tara looked at Jacky. "You chose to take over the day-to-day business. As far as I am concerned you are the right choice."

"I have to agree with Tara, Jacky. You can be our queen. King Arin is dying, and he has asked you for your hand, I suggest that you give it to him of your own free will."

Following the small ceremony Jacky spent most of her free time with King Arin, until he passed. A heclona later Jacky was crowned Queen of Geldania.

PART 2

GATHERING THE FLOCK

CHAPTER 9

SUSAN AND SAMANTHA

I t was January 1, 2041 at 2:00 am, 2,600 kilometers from the Sanctuary. Susan and Samantha sat at the table by the bar in their restaurant, each sipping from a glass of scotch. The New Year's party they had hosted was done and they had finished the basic clean up; the rest could wait.

"This time of year is the hardest since Mom and Dad passed," said Samantha.

They had both been devastated five years ago when two policemen arrived at the Rainbow restaurant early one morning. Diann, the maître d', had answered the door, but everyone in the kitchen heard her cry.

After the initial shock had worn off, and the weight of their grief diminished to where they could talk about their parents without breaking down, they decided they would run the family business, which they had inherited along with the house. They were both certified chefs, so with help from Paul, the sous chef, and his wife Diann the twins threw themselves into the business with a vengeance—probably as another way of dealing with their loss.

"Do you ever get the feeling that you have done everything you can do at this point in your life?" asked Susan.

Samantha shrugged. "Every day. By the way, I finished that book you gave me last month. It reminded me a lot of those dreams we've been having. In my dreams it seems as if I am right there, fighting alongside the Sorcerers, except my dreams are from a different perspective than the battles in *The Invasion of Geldania*. As if it was written by one of the Sorcerers who were there at the time maybe. But that's impossible isn't it? I think I could translate the funny glyphs on the front of the book, too. If I am right, they are co-ordinates to somewhere close to the Rocky Mountains in Alberta."

"Maybe we need to do something else for a while. I looked up the GPS co-ordinates as well. We always have been closely connected—always thinking the same things—although dreaming the same dreams takes it to a whole new level. Maybe you're on to something." Sue replied.

"Maybe this is that something we have been looking for," Sam suggested, "that something that captures our interest. Diann and Paul are more than capable of taking over here, and they have recently expressed an interest in having their own place."

"Let's figure this out Sam. First, we need to find out exactly where we are going on a map. With the information we have now we can do that easily enough." Sue said as she poured another shot.

"We haven't touched the money from Mom and Dad's insurance policy Sue, so we don't have to ask a fortune for this place, or the house for that matter. Something Paul and Diann can easily afford. Diann said she would like to start a family sooner than later."

"Okay, let's do this!" they said in unison.

Paul and Diann argued that the price was too low, saying they could come up with twice that.

"You're going to need that money as a cushion in case of unforeseen problems. Sue and I are okay with this. We have more than enough money to travel until we're ready to settle down again.

This place has too many memories, but we can take the good ones with us. We will be leaving when everything is finalized. You know that Sue and I love you both very much." Sam hugged each of them.

The paperwork took a week to complete, and the following morning Susan and Samantha loaded the last of what they were taking with them into the box of their three-quarter-ton 4-by-4 crew cab truck. Samantha closed the canopy door as Susan got into the driver's seat, and they began their trip to find what they hoped would be something new and exciting.

———∞◦〖◉〗◦∞———

It was the beginning of January. *It snowed again last night, but the weather channel said it would be sunny and warmer today,* Jason thought as he put two buckets of leftovers as feed for the pigs on one of the four-wheeled carts he had built. He cleared a path to the barn with a small whirl wind and started his chores. Jason put hay out for the cows, spread grains for the turkeys and chickens, and the mixture of various leftovers and vegetables went into the trough for the pigs. Then he collected eggs and milked the cows. It had been months since his book—*The Invasion of Geldania*—hit the shelves and he was beginning to wonder if Midnight might have been wrong in her judgment of the others.

———∞◦〖◉〗◦∞———

Samantha and Susan, dressed differently as usual, sat at a table in a hotel dining room eating breakfast. It was their fifth day traveling west, and the roads had been in reasonably good driving condition.

"How much further do you think we have to go Sam?"

"Four or five hours, if the weather holds. The locals say if you don't like the weather give it an hour 'cause it's sure to change." Susan laughed, but she didn't look happy at the thought.

They checked out of their room then drove to a gas bar where Samantha picked up a few snacks while Susan inquired about directions. It was tricky to ask for directions as the place that was indicated in the book was not on any map, even though they had a precise location locked-in to their GPS.

As the morning wore on the clouds to the west, directly in front of them, began to grow darker. They had been driving for about three hours when Susan pulled into the next gas station to see if they had charging stations.

"We better stop and charge the batteries up now. We still have another hundred kilometers to go and we might need to pull over if it starts to snow."

They had an early lunch and Samantha bought sandwiches and something to drink, just in case. It was her turn behind the wheel. Less than a half hour later they pulled into a roadside rest area to wait out the storm. The storm blew through fast and furious. When it stopped snowing, they sat looking at each other—continue or go back? A snowplow went by going in the direction they were headed, and Samantha chose to continue. They came to where they were supposed to turn off the main road onto a snow-covered secondary road.

"I don't think this is a good idea sis." Susan said, "We are way out here in the middle of nowhere with no snow tires. What if we get stuck?"

"We will be okay Sue; this truck has four-wheel drive. Relax, I got this." It was slow going but they made it to the co-ordinates the book had directed them to.

Jason finished the bookshelf he was building. It was a project he had been thinking of since he published his book and he had brought five boxes of books from his place in Edmonton on the last trip. Now he was building his library. If the others did come, which he was doubting, they would have plenty of books to choose from.

He was still getting used to moving things around using telekinesis, so it was going slower than he liked. *I could have done this faster by hand,* he thought when Midnight yelled …

———◦◦◦}◦◦{◦◦———

<JASON, SOMEONE IS COMING.>

Jason dropped the book he was shifting into position on a bookshelf.

"Damn it Midnight, you scared the hell out of me!"

He looked out the window. "I don't see anything Midnight."

<Whoever it is, trust me, they are coming. You need to develop your ability to see the magic of others young man. Think of how you know where I am, when you're out in the barn, or the greenhouse. Move across the room, close your eyes, and look with your mind. Do you see me sitting by the window?>

Jason did as Midnight requested.

"All right, I can sense you, and you have moved to the bookshelf. That was clever of you, and very funny Midnight. I still can't see anyone else."

<They are getting closer. Try expanding your perception toward the south east. You must push your mind further until you can SEE the magic of who is coming, see the magic they possess. I cannot say how far they are, but they are coming here.>

Jason had tried several times and was shaking his head in frustration when a pair of headlights appeared through the trees and stopped inside the tree line, back in the shadows.

"I can sense them now. I see two bodies inside that truck."

He looked at Midnight, expecting a response, but did not get one. Jason walked to the door.

<Jason, are you going to show them who you really are?>

Jason looked at her, then out at the truck. "I am Jason now, Midnight. Maybe sometime in the future, if I think it is worth telling them, I will share my story, but for now they are better off not knowing."

Susan and Samantha sat in their truck looking at the two-story building at the far end of the clearing. The door opened and a man with sandy blond hair stepped out and stood by the handrail, a black cat jumped up on the banister beside him. They stood there watching the truck.

"What do you make of this, Sam? We are way out in the middle of nowhere and we have a single male with his cat waiting for us to approach."

"This is the place we are supposed to be, Sue, and that's the guy who wrote the book. The GPS co-ordinates tell us this is the place. Let's see what he has to say before jumping to any wild conclusions."

Samantha put the truck in gear and drove slowly up to the building, parking beside the car already there.

The truck's doors opened, and a blonde woman stepped out of each door. Jason raised an eyebrow—twins. They both had sandy blond hair and sky-blue eyes that enhanced their beauty. "Good afternoon, ladies it is almost supper time. Would you like to come in for refreshments and conversation?"

They each closed their door and looked at each other before ascending the stairs. Jason opened the door. Midnight jumped down and entered first, the two women next, and Jason last.

"If you would like to freshen up, there are rooms upstairs with everything you should need. The rooms are all the same, so it doesn't matter which ones you chose."

The women nodded.

"I will get food ready while you do that."

The twins went upstairs, and Jason went into the kitchen. He loaded two of his four-wheeled carts with food, utensils, plates, and four pitchers. He set the table and waited for his guests to return. Midnight sat on her chair looking at Jason.

<You doubted me when I told you they would come; now the first ones are here. You're worried that they might react in the same way you did when I first told you about the gift of sorcery. I believe they will be skeptical at first, confused, and they might even leave. Believe in yourself Jason.>

"Explain to me why there are two. You told me you gave the gift to five other individuals."

<I cannot give you an answer to your question, because I don't have one. I intended the gift to go to Samantha.>

"Don't you think this is a bit strange Sam? I mean, why is he out here in the middle of nowhere?"

"Look at this room. It is more like an apartment than a hotel room. As for why, let's go down and ask him instead of worrying about it Sue."

Susan looked at her sister, not liking this one bit, but she shrugged her shoulders and followed Samantha out of the room.

When the twins entered the common room Midnight, seated in her usual chair, paid no attention to them. Jason stood and invited them to sit before he sat down again.

"You have me at a disadvantage. You know who I am, but I don't know who you are? Perhaps we could start with your names?"

The young woman closest to him replied. "I am Samantha, and this is my sister Susan. And yes, we do know who you are. You're the author of *The Invasion of Geldania* we both read. Why did you give us directions to this place, way out here in the middle of nowhere?"

"You will understand why I chose this place soon enough, but first we need to eat. Please help yourselves."

Susan and Samantha did that. Midnight sat and observed.

"Why did you choose such a remote place?" Samantha persisted.

Jason smiled. "All in good time. Do either of you recognize this cat? Midnight is her name and she is a unique cat, hard to forget. I met her about two years ago. She was covered in snow and half-frozen to death. She has been my companion ever since."

Susan frowned. "She looks like a cat we took in after our parents died, about five years ago. She was only with us a few months."

Jason nodded. "What I am going to tell you will sound unbelievable and you're probably going to think I am a nut case. I am not, but you will have to decide what to do with what you hear. Let me tell you Midnight's story.

"About three thousand years ago, on another world, there was a battle. As far as Midnight knows it was the final battle for freedom on a world called Orighen. Six Sorcerers, a dragon, and a cat from a breed of cats known as Furl Cats, confronted the leader of an army that was trying to take over their world. His name was Tay'Ron. Richard, one of the Sorcerers, and one of the best swordsmen from Geldania, fought with the evil Sorcerer Tay'Ron while Midnight and the other five Sorcerers kept his personal bodyguards at bay. The dragon, Scarlet, spewed fire over the heads of the enemy soldiers, giving them something else to worry about.

"Tay'Ron, as usual, was not playing by the rules. Both Richard and Tay'Ron had several wounds, and both were getting weary. Tay'Ron struck Richard down to the ground, and was about to deliver the killing blow, raising his sword with both hands over his head, when Richard getting to one knee thrust his sword up under Tyron's chain mail and into his heart. Tay'Ron had enough time left to cast one last spell, sending Richard, Midnight, and the other Sorcerers to another world: this world.

"Tay'Ron also introduced a virus into the spell that infected all of them. It was years before they discovered they had it, however, and try as they might they could find no cure. Approximately three hundred years passed before they began dying.

"Midnight is a creature of magic, and she has the ability to absorb the gift from one who is dying. She was able to store each of their gifts separately inside herself. Perhaps that is why she still lives today, thousands of years later.

"...Midnight found the two of you and decided you were worthy of possessing one of these gifts, so she gave you something others can only dream of having. Midnight gave you the gift of sorcery."

Susan and Samantha looked at Jason, eyes wide, and then looked across the table at Midnight.

"Do you really think we are going to believe this bullshit? Your story is very touching, but you *are* a writer. This sounds like it belongs in one of your novels. Come Sam, I think it's time we left." Susan said.

<You have good reason to doubt what you hear Susan. On this world, sorcery is considered, by most, to be fantasy fiction. I am Midnight and I converse through telepathy. On my world, magic is a common thing. Jason has told my story truthfully, and I understand that it scares you to think that it might be true. Take some time; think about what you've heard, discuss it together.>

Both women stood, glared at Jason and Midnight, and turned toward the door.

"I have a question you should think about before leaving. Why did the two of you come here?" Jason asked.

The twins gave him a sour look before walking out the door.

"That went like you expected. What do we do now? Sit here and wait?"

<They will not leave, trust me. You had doubts about sorcery when I first talked to you didn't you? They are scared as you were.

This knowledge is not easy to comprehend, as you know. Give them time to talk about what they heard here.>

Jason didn't argue with her as he gathered up the remains of their meal, putting everything on the carts. Once he was finished putting leftovers away, he sat down and concentrated on locating the twins.

Jason found Midnight easily; she was in the other room, probably looking out the window. He detected two more spots of magic outside. The twins were sitting in their truck, and hopefully discussing what they had been told.

"Sue, we can't just leave," Samantha said. "He is right to ask, why did we come? We walked away from everything to come here looking for answers to questions we needed answered. We came looking for something new, something different. This is beyond our wildest dreams. At least we can, maybe, look around, and give this some more thought."

"Sam, I'm scared. Sorcery? Who would have thought that this was even possible? Am I wrong to be skeptical?"

Samantha didn't answer. She needed more information, and they were not going to get it sitting in the truck.

"Come on Sue, there's a road over there that goes to that barn we saw from the upper window. Let's see what's in there."

Samantha backed the truck up and drove to the barn, noticing that the road was clear of snow. When they entered, overhead lights came on to reveal a large space with exercise equipment. Susan looked up at the lighting—globes of light suspended in midair, no visible wires. *That's impossible,* she thought. A cow mooed, a pig grunted; they walked toward these sounds, lights coming on as they moved. What they saw stunned them. The back of the barn had to be two hundred yards away.

"What in hell is going on here? How can the inside be so much larger than the outside?" Samantha swallowed hard.

"The magic of sorcery allows us to defy certain rules. We can create things with a thought. Change things, like the inside of the barn. Make anything that you can buy, anything you can imagine, within reason." Jason stepped out of one of the cow stalls with a bucket of milk—chores still needed to be done—and he looked at the two white-faced women.

"I apologize for scaring you. In the winter, and the unpredictable weather throughout the year, the animals and fowl need adequate space to move around. The barn was too small, so I had to give them more room."

Susan and Samantha looked at him as if they were seeing him for the first time.

"I ask you to trust Midnight and me. We mean you no harm. However, the choice to unlock the gift is yours. If you choose not to, there is no foul. You will probably live a much longer life than you would have naturally. However, if you choose to unlock the gift, once you awaken the spark inside you, you can't undo that procedure. With the proper training, you would be able to create what you have seen here and much more. You're welcome to stay here while you make your decision. That too is your choice, and we will not try and stop you if you decide to leave." Jason turned and left the barn.

Samantha and Susan followed him out of the barn and watched Jason take a trail a short way down the road. Still wanting to explore, Susan returned the truck to the parking area in front of the main house then walked back to Samantha at the trail. The greenhouse caught their attention.

"Wow, this place is huge. This is a chef's dream, Sue."

Susan gave Samantha a sour look. She was still not sure they should stay. They walked around the greenhouse looking at the plants.

The chef in Susan was intrigued though. "He has everything here. Plants you can only find in specialty stores, and every kind of vegetable, herb—even edible flowers. Do you think he did all this with this gift, with this sorcery?"

Samantha shook her head. "I doubt that he was able to do all this without something we can't explain Sue. Let's go back to the house."

As they followed the walkway around to the front. Susan looked at her sister.

"You think we should go along with this, don't you Sam? Why?"

"We came here looking for adventure, sis; a change to our lives, a new journey, a new beginning, a rebirth. I would say we most definitely have found it, wouldn't you? We can't deny the dreams either. Jason looks somewhat like Richard, and you know that what we have heard here today reflects those dreams, so let's go upstairs and get some rest, think this through. We can decide what to do in the morning."

They grabbed their overnight bags from the truck before turning back to the house.

When they entered, Jason had his back to the door and was putting books in the bookshelf by floating them through the air. Midnight was nowhere to be seen. Jason did not look at them as they continued up the stairs.

Midnight let out a sigh. <See Jason? I told you they would stay.>

"You saw that! That cannot be a trick." Samantha said. "We have the means already, all we have to do is say yes, Sue."

—∘∘⋙◉⋘∘∘—

The twins woke to the smell of cooking bacon, and coffee, wafting through the hallways. They had decided to share one room for the night, as they had talked long after turning out the light.

As Susan and Samantha entered the common room, Jason, who had sensed them coming, wheeled the cart filled with food and drink through the swinging doors.

"You are still here I see. And you look like you need some coffee."

Samantha looked at him with a sheepish grin and sat down; Susan sat beside her, her face pale. There was plenty of food—loaves of fresh baked bread with butter and jam, bacon and eggs, jugs of orange juice and milk fresh from the cow, and lots of coffee. Midnight sat in her chair with her bowl of milk and a plate of food.

"Was your room suitable? Is there anything you need?"

"The room is fine. We would like to apologize for our reaction yesterday. What you told us is a lot to take in, a lot to process in a short period of time. Sam and I came here because we both needed a change; our parents were killed in a car accident, and we had to get out of that place—too many bad memories. After Midnight left, if she is the same cat that stayed with us, we began having dreams. Reading your book was like seeing those dreams from a different angle.

"The battles, the people, and the events in your book matched our dreams, so that helped us to make the decision to follow your sign. We left everything behind: our home, our business, and our friends. The past five years have been hard on us, so we came in search of something new, something different."

Samantha stood up. "How does this work?"

Jason looked at Susan. She nodded her agreement to proceed.

"Before we go on, there's something you need to know. I told you that I found Midnight in a snowbank, half-frozen. What I didn't tell you is, that, at the time I was 89 years old, and dying of a severe lung disease. Because too many people already knew this, I had to die. Midnight and I faked my death, and I became Jason Blain. My name is DeWayne Richards and that is who I was. Jason is the life I chose, the person DeWayne became when he died."

The twins' jaws dropped as Jason turned into an old man with long white hair and beard reaching down to his waist.

"This is a small thing you will be able to do as well. Change your appearance that is. However, that is not something either of you need to do."

He smiled as he changed back. "You have already had a good meal, so now each of you will lie on one of these couches and I touch your forehead so I can find your gift and turn it on, like turning on a light. You will be disoriented for a short time—how long, I cannot honestly say."

Susan frowned. "Does it hurt? Will it change us?"

"No, there is no pain. Trust me, you will be the same as you are now, except you will be one step closer to being a Sorcerer. We will have more food ready for you to aid in your recovery. This does take a lot of energy. Midnight and I will be here watching over you the whole time. You have nothing to fear. Do you have any more questions?"

"No, we are ready for this," Samantha said.

Jason moved two of the couches together with enough room to walk between them. Susan and Samantha each sat down on a couch and stretched out, hands folded across their chests.

Jason touched Susan's forehead first and unlocked her gift, then did the same for Samantha. Jason moved a chair to the end of the couches as Midnight jumped up onto the back of one, her long tail swaying back and forth.

It wasn't quite three hours later when Susan began to fidget, and only seconds later Samantha did as well. Jason knelt on the floor between them, softly telling them that everything was okay. He talked them through the worst of the confusion. When they had mostly recovered, he helped them to the table and placed food in front of them, then watched as they both ate. They ate slowly at first, but the food worked quickly.

"I feel so much better, and now I am ready to start learning," Samantha said with a smile.

Susan looked at her. "I do feel better, but maybe we should rest for a while."

Jason said, "Susan is right; you should rest for a bit, but I will give you something to think about while you're doing that." He stood and touched each of them on the forehead for a second.

"What is this, you can look into our minds?" Susan asked.

"No, I cannot read or look into your minds," Jason said. "That is one of the things Sorcerers cannot do. I have only placed a short thought of mine in your mind. This is the way in which Midnight and I will teach you. A touch, and thoughts are transferred."

Samantha looked at Jason. "I received your thought, almost like series of images, so we just learn what they mean?"

"Yes, Samantha. You take what I have given you and you learn and understand what it means. Once you have done that, you have to reach inside yourself—meditation is how I achieved that part—find your gift, the spark that is inside you, and then make it a part of yourself—complete the connection—touch it with your mind. This is something you need to do individually, as far as I know. Right now, the gift is there, and awake, but it still needs to connect with you, so you and it can become one."

The twins rose and went upstairs. Midnight gave Jason a searching look before she spoke.

<Many years ago, while I was traveling north along the western side of the inland mountains, I sensed something that contained, or was made with magic. It was high up in the mountain. I cannot tell you where it was exactly, but I can give you my visual memories. Otherwise, you're going to have to travel the highway to the south of here, going west through the mountains and then go north till you find the place.

<You might want to take Samantha and Susan with you on this quest. They seem to know what the other is thinking—maybe something to do with them being twins—which might double their powers of observation. This is one of those things I was holding back until the time was right.>

Jason nodded his head. "You are suggesting we go on a quest to find this magical whatever it is? Is there anything else you would like to share with me?"

Midnight only looked at him as if to say, not right now.

"Okay, give me your mental images and I will see what I can do with them."

Midnight jumped up on his lap and placed her paw to his cheek, then went back to her preferred chair. Jason found his sketch pad and put the images to paper. With sorcery, his artistic abilities were enhanced. He would scan the images into his computer and use a program to find real life places with similar geographical or topographical profiles.

Samantha looked at Susan, "What do you think he means by 'you have to touch your gift'? Isn't that what he just did?"

Sue shook her head. "I don't know, but it sounds like he's telling us to meditate, to look inside and see if we can find this spark. That is the only thing I can think of. Let's try that after we figure out this lesson he gave us. To me it is a confusing jumble of images. One shows him reading someone's mind and the next one is the same with an X. I am guessing that means no mind reading. The next one is him making a flower, then destroying it, and he explodes. The next series shows the flower, it becomes a spoon, and he is smiling. The last one has me confused though. What do think that means Sam?"

"We can make something with magic and change it into something else but we can't destroy it with magic. Or maybe you just can't destroy anything made with magic? The last one tells me we should not kill unless there is no other solution. Not much on rules so lets try this meditation thingy."

The twins sat on the bed facing each other and concentrated on their gifts individually. Nothing happened.

Then they realized they could connect their minds with the gift, so they decided to do it their way instead. They connected their minds and went deep within. Finding the spark in each other was easy enough. Touching it took a few attempts but eventually they figured it out.

Over the next month Samantha and Susan learned from both Jason and Midnight. They started with the basics, as Jason had, like making an edible tomato and other useful items. Then they learned how to use magic to enhance their cooking and how to converse telepathically with Jason and Midnight—although the humans still defaulted to verbal speech most of the time.

They also helped with the farm chores, including gathering eggs and milking the cows. Jason showed them how to make cheese and butter, and they studied the residents of the barn so they could reproduce the meat for meals.

ADAM AND AMANDA

I t was the last week in January when Amanda walked into the house she shared with her twin brother and tossed her boots into the closet. She stalked into the living room, sighed, and poured herself a drink.

"Hi, sis. Sounds like you had another bad day?" Adam said.

"Not bad. Every day is the same, over and over, day in and day out. I need a change. We need a change. Ever since Mom and Dad passed away, everything has been different, and living here only keeps the bad memories at the forefront. You said as much yourself the other day, Adam."

Their parents' car had been t-boned by a drunk driver who ran a red light, killing them instantly. It was over seven years ago now. At the time, moving back in to the family home together had seemed like a good idea, but every day was a reminder of their loss.

"Yeah, I know sis. Bring me one of those will you?" Adam said indicating the drink in her hand. "I finished that book you gave me; the one that reminded you of those dreams we've been having.

Dreams that began after the stray black cat they cared for, for two months, suddenly disappeared.

"I have to wonder if you found anything strange, like the rune writing on the cover."

Amanda downed her drink, refilled her glass and poured one for Adam.

"You read the same thing I did? The symbols—I understood what they said. They are directions to a place in Alberta, in the foothills this side of the mountains."

"Yeah, I checked and got the same results. I think we should go there and find out why we were able to read that in the first place. January is a slow time at the bistro for you, and it's the calm before the storm of tax season for my accounting firm. We can take leaves of absence and get out of here for a while!" Adam smiled as he took a sip of his drink.

"We both agree that we cannot stay here any longer. We might as well sell the damn place and plan for a trip west."

After a minute's thought Adam agreed with her. They wrote letters of resignation, giving their employers two weeks' notice. Adam put the house up for sale at under market value, figuring it would sell faster that way. They both had more than enough money, so proceeds from the sale were a bonus. The house sold three weeks later, and the paperwork took another week. Adam and Amanda packed items that they wanted from the house, loaded everything into the back of Adam's truck, and left the following day.

Susan and Samantha were using telekinesis to organize books, which Jason had scattered around the room, onto the bookshelves when they sensed someone with the gift coming.

"How far away are they?" Jason asked.

<Whoever it is, they should be here in about fifteen minutes.> Midnight answered.

"Sam, Sue, please put your culinary skills to work and prepare a nice meal for our guest, if you wouldn't mind."

Jason looked at Midnight. Her stance told him something was wrong. Jason went outside to welcome this newcomer, with Midnight right behind him.

—∘○⟨◉⟩○∘—

Amanda could see a large building through the trees.

"We are here, Adam. I can see a building up ahead."

Before they left the cover of the trees, Adam stopped the truck.

"Someone is standing on that walkway in front of the house, and there's a cat standing on the handrail. Everything looks okay. What do you think sis?"

Amanda was staring at the person standing on the porch.

"That's the author of *The Invasion of Geldania*."

Just then two women came out and joined the man, who was now leaning on the handrail beside the cat.

"Are we going to sit here watching them or are we going over there?" Amanda asked.

"This place does look a bit intimidating when you're sitting out there looking in," Samantha said as they watched the truck begin moving again.

The truck stopped beside Susan and Samantha's truck. A man and woman, both with black hair, stepped out of the truck. They looked a lot alike.

"Hello, I am Jason Blain. The twins have made lunch. Come in and join us."

The new arrivals walked up the stairs as Jason opened the door. "Sit down. We can eat, talk, and get to know each other."

Amanda and Adam sat down surveying the variety of sliced meats, breads, vegetables, salads, cheeses, and pickles, along with several different beverages, sitting on the table.

"I suppose we should introduce ourselves. I am Adam and this is my sister Amanda. We're twins if you hadn't noticed."

"Adam and I read your book and realized we were able to read the symbols, and interpret their meaning, so now we are here. Can you explain it to us? What's going on?"

"As I told you before I am Jason. More twins, how interesting," Jason said, looking at Midnight.

"Susan and Samantha have been here for about a month now." Jason indicated the twins with a wave of his hand. "And last, but definitely not least, I present Midnight the Furl Cat from Orighen."

Adam looked at Amanda wondering what in hell was he talking about.

Jason asked if they recognized Midnight. When they agreed that she might be the cat they had taken in several years ago, Jason asked if they would like to hear Midnight's story.

"This is not the big cat from our dreams is she? Maybe her story will give us answers to questions we have as well," Adam said.

Jason reached the end of the story as they finished the meal. He looked at Adam and Amanda. "There are rooms upstairs if you would like to take some time to digest your meal, and what you have heard here. Perhaps Sue or Sam can show you the way."

Amanda looked at him. "Everything you have told us we know nothing about. We have had no dreams that support what you're telling us. Can you explain that?"

Susan looked at her. "Sam and I asked ourselves that same question. The only answer we can come up with is that our dreams have not progressed that far yet. Or maybe they never were." Samantha stood up. "Come on. Sue and I will give you a tour of our house."

Adam looked at his sister, shrugged, and the four of them left the table while Jason cleaned up the remnants of the meal.

"It seems your idea is working, Midnight. Do you think Adam and Amanda will stay as well?"

<They will stay. I am more concerned that this is the second time that two have come instead of one. I cannot explain why they

both received the gift on two occasions. Maybe I will never know how that happened.>

"If I may make an observation, you don't know much about twins, do you? They have a unique bond, which you have already seen in Samantha and Susan, although it is usually stronger in identical twins like they are. Giving the gift to one may have inadvertently given it to both; same thing goes for Adam and Amanda. They seem to be as close as brother and sister as Samantha and Susan are."

<Do you believe that is the reason they both received the gift? Can this bond between siblings be that powerful? That might be a reasonable assumption, I will do some research on the matter. Susan and Samantha are close to their age, and they will be able to answer the questions that they will ask.

<Right now, we have to concentrate our efforts on finding my mountain. Have you finished the revised sketches yet? Maybe I can look them over to make sure they are as I remember them.>

Midnight's memory was foggy, and Jason had had to redo them several times. However, each time he did Midnight seemed to remember more details. Jason brought the folder out and the two of them began critiquing the most recent sketches one by one.

"You understand, Midnight, that we can't do anything right now. Adam and Amanda are not ready for an excursion like this. Even after they accept the gift, they have to learn how to use it before we can even begin to make plans to go on this quest."

<There are other things I need to do once it is completed. Maybe I should say that you have to do, because I am not strong enough.>

"Spring is not that far off; however, we are in the foothills and a heavy snowfall is common this close to the mountains. Midnight, you know that trying to complete this quest at this time of year would be futile, not to mention extremely dangerous. You have me looking for someplace I have never been, and you will have me and at least a couple of others climbing mountains. I have to wonder what other secrets you're keeping."

Midnight didn't respond.

They worked on the sketches until Susan, Samantha, Adam, and Amanda came downstairs. They did not stop to talk, but walked through the kitchen and out the back door.

Susan walked beside Amanda. "This place is much more than it seems. Your room is larger than the building allows. Once you see things from the outside you will understand."

"Look at the greenhouse; it doesn't look like much from the outside does it? Samantha opened the door and they entered. Adam's eyes widened as he took in the view.

"How is this possible? This is ten times larger inside than it is outside."

"This is magic!" Sue said quietly. "We harvest what is needed for every meal from here. There is more than enough for us plus a dozen more. What we don't use goes to feed the livestock and fowl."

Amanda frowned. "Livestock? Where do you keep them?"

Samantha said, "Come, that is our next stop. The barn isn't far!"

"We do not use them for food, except the eggs and the milk. The animals are here for study purposes only." Samantha continued the tour.

Amanda walked toward the critters.

"If you don't use them for food then where does the meat come from?"

Samantha turned and looked at them.

"We study them, and with our gift we can reproduce the meat exactly, even fully cooked when we are in a hurry. The eggs on the other hand are there for the taking. The milk we drink and make into butter and cheese. We do not waste what is readily available."

Susan turned and walked toward the door.

"We have shown you the benefits of having the gift, now it is up to you to decide if you want to take the next step and bring your gift fully to life or return to the life you left behind. It is beautiful here, right by the mountains."

As they walked back to the house, Adam and Amanda fell back and talked quietly.

"We need to talk about this, in private, before we make a decision," Adam said as they reached the house.

Amanda and her brother went up to their room. Jason asked the twins how things had gone with the newcomers.

"They are fascinated with what we have here. They were in awe at the fact that most of it was created with magic, and a bit intimidated at the same time I believe. We have to give them time to digest what they have learned here today," Susan said.

Jason nodded. "When they decide to stay, are the two of you confident enough with the knowledge you have received to join in their training?"

Samantha looked at him. "You want us to help with their training as well?"

"Susan, Samantha, the two of you have earned the right to move on. Are you ready to take the next step? Remember, when it comes time for them to learn, they need to learn as you did, no helping where helping is not needed," Jason said. "Can you awaken their gift when they decide to move forward, or do you want me to handle that?"

"That is a big step Jason." Samantha paused.

Sue interjected. "We can do that."

"I guess Sue knows more than I do at this time." Samantha grinned.

Jason smiled in response. "The two of you are a part of our family now, and you have built a rapport with Adam and Amanda. They will be comfortable learning from the two of you—and Midnight and I are here if you have any problems."

Samantha looked at her sister. "I am sure that with some guidance from you and Midnight we can learn how to teach like you do."

Jason was satisfied with that answer and motioned for them to follow him to the kitchen. They finished preparing the meal and Susan called up to Adam and Amanda that food was on the table.

"You sure eat frequently," said Amanda as they entered the common room.

Samantha laughed. "Using magic requires a lot of energy, so we need to refuel often."

Adam sat beside Amanda and they ate the meal in silence. As they finished Adam spoke. "Amanda and I have decided to stay and activate this spark or gift you spoke of. What happens now? How do we proceed?"

"Samantha and Susan will look for the gift inside each of you and bring it to life. There will be a short time, maybe two or three hours, where your body will be absorbing the gift. One of us will be here watching over you the whole time. This does take a lot of energy, so we will have another meal ready when you wake. If Susan and Samantha find they need help, I will be standing by to assist. When that part is done you move onto step two, but first things first."

Adam lay on one couch and Amanda on the other. Susan placed her hand on Adam's forehead and closed her eyes. Adam's eyes opened wide when she brought his gift to life.

Samantha touched Amanda's forehead, repeating the process with her. It was just under three hours later when Adam began to fidget, and only a short time after that Amanda began coming around. Susan and Samantha moved closer to Amanda and Adam, reassuring them that they were doing fine.

Jason went to the dining table and prepared another meal. Adam, disoriented, managed to sit up with a little help from Susan. Amanda needed a bit more help sitting up. Samantha spoke softly to them encouraging them to get up and walk to the table where food and drink awaited them. The blonde twins helped their dark-haired charges to the table.

As they ate Amanda and Adam became more responsive, and eager to move to the next step, much like Susan and Samantha had.

"You were right; eating has made me feel much better. What's next?" Amanda asked.

"Susan and I will help you with that. There are challenges that must be met as you move forward. Because we have already met those challenges, we can give you some guidance. However, most of your learning must be done by yourselves."

The four of them went off to talk in private.

Once he had cleaned up the dining room, Jason scanned the newest drawings into his computer. While that computer was searching for the mountain, he began a new search on another computer for something else that had caught his interest.

The first computer pinged, letting Jason know that the first search was complete. Jason saved those results and began a new search with the second drawing. He did the same for all the drawings until all the sketches had been searched. This time he had several possible locations. By cross-referencing he was able to accurately pinpoint the mountain they were looking for.

Early the next morning as Jason was preparing breakfast, the four twins entered the kitchen. To his surprise they took over the preparations, telling Jason to go sit down. He didn't argue. Midnight joined Jason at the table.

<You found what we are looking for? When do you think you can go?>

"Yes, I found one mountain that matches the drawings. It is probably the one we are looking for; however, it may not be the one. I have the co-ordinates and a map showing us the way. When we can go is not up to me Midnight, it's depends on the weather."

<I don't like it, but I do understand. Losing the three of you would defeat my efforts to bring you all together.>

Susan and Amanda brought out the first cart of food with Adam and Samantha close behind with another. When they finished the meal, Jason inquired how things were going.

Adam cleared his throat. "Amanda and I have completed the first challenge and are working on the next one."

"I am pleased to hear that. It seems that Susan and Samantha were the right choice," Jason said smiling.

CHAPTER 11

FRANK AND MARIE

Marie locked the door to the clinic. She picked up the two suitcases and walked to the motorhome where she lived with her husband Frank. They were both doctors and had left their private practice in Vancouver four years ago, just after that stray cat had decided to move on. For some reason neither of them could explain they bought the motorhome and took their practice on the road—maybe it was the cat leaving. They had visited small towns and villages that didn't have a doctor in residence, First Nation reserves, and wherever else their help was needed.

Before they left Yellowknife—after a three-week locum for a friend—they restocked their medical supplies and food. Marie also took a well-earned break to peruse the speculative fiction aisle of the bookstore. *The Invasion of Geldania* caught her attention. The glyphs on the cover looked familiar to her.

———◦∘⦂◉⦂∘◦———

March was ending; Adam and Amanda were progressing well. It was mid-morning when Midnight ran to the front windows and jumped up on a chair.

<Susan, Samantha, I am detecting a presence coming this way. Can you confirm that?>

Midnight knew the twins had a unique ability for sensing the gift in others at a distance. Susan looked at Adam with a raised eyebrow. She could see that Adam and Amanda were both concentrating as well.

"Yes, there is a magical presence coming this way. Ten or fifteen minutes maybe?" Adam looked at the two sisters for confirmation.

"Yes, you are getting better at this," Susan said with a huge smile.

Jason understood that Susan and Samantha had a certain bond with Adam and Amanda. *Another one comes*, he thought. *Maybe they will all be here sooner than later?*

The walkway in front of the house had five humans leaning on the handrail, and one black cat sitting on it. Jason was surprised when a large mobile home came out of the trees and continued up to the Sanctuary.

An older man and woman stepped out of the motorhome. "Good morning," they said simultaneously to those standing on the walkway.

"And we wish a good morning to both of you as well. Come in so we can sit and chat. I am sure we can provide refreshments as well," Jason said with a smile.

The newcomers followed Jason and the others into the house. They sat at the table while Susan and Samantha put on their chef-hats to prepare a meal. Jason made small talk until the twins came in with the food.

Jason introduced his family and waited for a reply.

"I am Frank, and this is my lovely wife, Marie. We are both doctors and have been traveling, helping where help is needed. When we read your book and found your message we decided to check into it further."

"I have a question for both of you. Have you ever seen Midnight before?" Jason asked. "She is a member of our family as well."

"We did take a cat in while we still lived in Vancouver, and Midnight certainly looks a lot like that cat, so I would have to say yes," Marie said.

"You will probably find what I am about to tell you hard to believe, but everything I say is true," Jason said as he began his narrative.

"… Midnight has found those she deemed worthy, and some of them are sitting here. Each of you received a gift. How that happened I cannot say, only Marie was supposed to receive it, yet here you both are. But Midnight only gave you the gift, it still needs to be awakened. That is where we come in. Samantha and Susan will guide Adam and Amanda in the process that will unlock your gift, if you wish to do so. Only you can make that decision though. There are rooms upstairs if you would like to think this over, or I'm sure the twins would be happy to show you around."

Frank looked at Marie. "Do you mind if we take a walk around the grounds and think this over?"

"Of course, take whatever time you need. We're all here to answer any questions you may have."

"Thanks, but I think Frank and I need to do this on our own," Marie said.

Jason and the others watched as the two older folks walked out the front door. Susan stood up and started to go after them.

Jason motioned everyone to stay seated. "Give Frank and Marie the time they need."

Jason could sense Frank and Marie as they explored the grounds.

"You have quite an interesting place here," Marie said when they returned to the common room. "We checked your greenhouse and barn—very impressive. We can see that this gift you speak of has many uses. We'd like to talk with the twins, all four of them, if that is all right with you?"

"You do not need my permission to speak with the others. There are few rules here, and they only apply to the use of sorcery. I believe the twins are in the kitchen," Jason told Marie.

Frank and Marie were greeted with smiling faces when they entered the kitchen. "It appears that you are treated well here. The food is excellent. Tell us, what is it like living here?" Frank asked.

Susan went over to the table in the corner and pulled out a chair for Marie.

"The food is excellent because it is always fresh. The rooms are apartments on the inside, and they are fully furnished. You have walked around the property, so you know it is beautiful here. We learn by doing what it is we are supposed to be learning. Jason or Midnight give us a lesson, and we need to figure out how it works. Being here is more like a vacation than a school; it's our Sanctuary."

Marie sipped from the glass of wine Adam had given her. "We have walked around the property, seen things we don't understand. Tell us, how does this works?"

Samantha sat down. "Once we decided to stay, Jason unlocked our gift, but that was only the beginning. After he activated the gift, he told us we had to personally connect with it, make it a part of ourselves."

"Does it hurt when he activates the gift? Will it interfere with the knowledge we already have? Is it going to change who we are?" Worry creased Frank's brow.

"It does not hurt, but you will be disoriented for a short while after the process is complete. There has been no change in who we are and as far our knowledge goes, it has only been enhanced, not altered," Amanda said confidently.

Frank and Marie got up and went out the back door.

"What do you think, Frank? Do we stay, or do we go?"

"It seems to be too good to be true, but we have seen things that contradict that, so yes we should stay. We already have this gift inside us, so we might as well use it to our advantage. If we can apply this sorcery to our knowledge of medicine…think for a moment what that could mean."

Marie looked at her husband, nodding her head. They returned to the kitchen and told the twins and Jason, who was also waiting for them, that they were going to stay.

Jason ushered everyone back to the common room. "There will be someone with you throughout the process. It takes approximately three hours and a lot of energy. Are you ready to begin?"

Susan took Amanda's hand and placed it on Marie's forehead. Amanda could see the spark that was the gift, and with Susan's guidance she touched it, bringing it awake. Samantha did the same with Adam and Frank.

Jason sat in a chair close by, checking his map of the trip they would be taking to Midnight's mountain on his laptop. There had been a storm along the route, which had dumped a considerable amount of snow. He hoped it would be melted by the time they were ready to leave.

Jason looked up when someone called his name. Marie and Frank were coming around. Susan and Samantha had gone to prepare a meal, but Adam was standing by the couches with an anxious look on his face.

Jason touched his arm. "Call your sister and we will do this together."

Amanda came out of the kitchen. With Jason's guidance the twins helped Frank and Marie sit up and then steadied them as they walked to the table. Marie and Frank improved when the meal was finished. Adam and Amanda took the older couple upstairs to one of the rooms to rest and complete their transition to Sorcerers.

Over the next three weeks, Frank and Marie learned how to use their new powers and started teaching medical care to the others, including Jason.

CHAPTER 12

BOBBY JOE AND JOHNATHAN

B obby Joe picked up a pen and wrote down the directions she had found on the cover of *The Invasion of Geldania*. Such interesting books came to her attention as head librarian at one of the larger libraries in North Bay. With her mother and father both being only children as she was, she was the last of her family line.

She sat in her office and let her mind wander. *Why am I able to read these hieroglyphics? They are unlike any I have studied in the past.* She was only forty-five years old, but she did want more from life—like living out her recent dreams. She laughed at herself.

But still, she did a search for the co-ordinates on her computer and found that they were in Alberta, about 3100 kilometers away.

Is this what I've been looking for? Something new and exciting like the dreams.

Decision made, Bobby Joe handed in her resignation at the library and began the process of selling her home. The library was city property and the councilor for that district asked her why she was leaving. She explained as best she could. "The farthest I have ever been from home is Toronto. I read about the Rocky

Mountains and I am told that the pictures do them no justice. I want to travel, while I still can. I want to see those mountains up close; I want to dip my toes into the Pacific Ocean. Isn't that reason enough?" She packed what she wanted to keep into her car and let the rest go with the sale of the house.

Johnathan signed the papers for the deed on his house in the small town of Ferguson Cove in Nova Scotia. He had everything he wanted from the house already packed and in his truck's box. John wasn't in any hurry to get to Alberta; after all he was taking his first real holiday in five years. He was an engineer, and his work had kept him away from home for many months at a time.

Johnathan intended on traveling west at a tourist's pace, stopping at places that he had always wanted to see. He wasn't sure what to expect when he arrived at his destination, but he felt deep down inside that this might be his last trip.

Bobby Joe stopped for the night. After she had checked into her room, she went down to the restaurant and bar for something to eat. As she walked down the aisle, she dropped her room key. A dark-skinned man sitting at the table next to her picked her key up, and with a pleasant smile, handed it to her. She thanked him and continued to an empty table. After Bobby Joe had finished her meal she retired to her room.

John watched as the black-haired woman left the dining room. *It seems that girl's mind is someplace else. Oh well, so is mine.* He called it a night and went to his room.

Susan jumped up from her chair. "Someone is coming, Midnight, Sam, Adam, Amanda, do you sense them?"

"There are two different somebodies coming. Maybe ten minutes apart. We should get ready to greet them," Adam said.

Jason stood outside on the raised walkway with the others. The first vehicle slowed, but didn't stop at the tree line. It drove up to the building. A black-haired woman stepped out of the car.

Samantha smiled at her. "You are welcome here. Come in; we have food and beverages waiting for you."

Just then the other vehicle came through the trees. A man with dark skin and dark brown curly hair stepped out of a truck. When he saw the black-haired woman, he smiled and gave a gentleman's bow to her. "We meet again."

Jason saw the same confusion on the faces of the others as he felt at this comment, but he said nothing.

"You are both welcome here, so why don't we go inside where it is warmer, where good food and drink await us all."

They sat at the table and introductions were made. As they ate, the two newcomers told them a little bit about themselves. When the meal was done Jason asked them if they remembered Midnight. When Bobby Joe and Johnathan admitted that they did remember a cat that looked a lot like Midnight, Jason asked, "Would you like to hear Midnight's story?"

"She took the gift of all six Sorcerers into herself," Jason concluded the story. "And when she could no longer continue to look for a cure, she decided that she had to find people who were worthy of receiving the gifts she had to give. Both of you met that criterion. Midnight gave you each the gift; now it is up to you to decide if you want to take the next step to become a Sorcerer."

"This may be hard for you to believe right now, so take some time to absorb what you have heard today. There are rooms upstairs. Susan and I will take you up and show you the ones that are not taken yet," said Samantha.

"Perhaps Frank, Marie, Amanda, and I should go up too?" Adam said, and followed them upstairs, the others close behind him.

Midnight jumped up on the chair beside Jason.

<The days are getting warmer and the snow is melting. How much longer before you go on your quest?>

"We should see how things go with our newcomers first. Let's wait and see what the weather looks like at the end of the month. I understand your concern, but if we go too soon, we have a chance of getting stuck somewhere along the way. Waiting for things to dry out enough so we can continue could take days. You know what it is like when you're traveling at this time of year."

Jason scratched one of Midnight's ears. Everything had already been planned for the quest to the mountains. The days *were* getting warmer, and the snow was melting, but he had seen the weather change overnight before, with the sun shining and melting the snow one day, and ten inches of snow the next.

Hours later Bobby Joe and Johnathan came downstairs. The rest of the family gathered to hear the verdict. Bobby Joe looked at Jason.

"We are ready to take the next step. It seems we both knew in the back of our minds that this would be our last stop."

Jason looked at Frank. "Would you and Marie like to do the honors? Adam and Amanda will guide you. As you told us about learning medical procedures, 'see one, do one, teach one' is the best way to learn."

Frank and Marie accompanied Bobby Joe and Johnathan to the couches. Marie directed the two newcomers to lie down as Adam and Amanda joined them.

Jason prepared a meal as Bobby Joe and Johnathan came around, weak and disoriented. Frank sat beside John, and Marie beside Bobby Joe, reassuring them that everything was as it should be. They helped the two get to their feet and then to the dining table. When the meal was finished Amanda and Adam took Marie and Frank, Bobby Joe, and Johnathan with them upstairs to help Bobby and John get past the first hurdle.

Over the next week Bobby Joe and Johnathan learned as quickly as the others had. At first, they didn't see the need for the exercise equipment, nor practicing with swords, throwing knives, and learning how to use a bow and arrows. By the second day it became clear to them, that having the gift of sorcery did not keep your body in shape.

The household settled into a routine of training, learning, and chores as the weather continued its progression toward spring.

CHAPTER 13

THE QUEST

As April slipped into May, Midnight again asked Jason if it was time to go on the quest.

"Yes, it seems that spring is settling in well. I will discuss it with the others tonight. Our route has already been planned, so we can leave tomorrow."

The evening meal was the one time that all ten of them gathered together in the common room. It was a time to discuss the day's challenges and successes. Tonight, was slightly different.

"Several years ago, Midnight found something magical hidden on the west side of the Rocky Mountains. She was unable to check it out herself due to her deteriorating condition. I am going to retrieve it, whatever it is. I'd like Susan and Samantha to come with me on this journey, if you will." Jason paused and looked at the twins. "You were the first to arrive here, so you are more advanced in your training."

Samantha and Susan both nodded their assent to the plan.

Jason continued. "Midnight will be your teacher until I return. Other than adjusting for chores, your training can continue as it has been, with Midnight teaching Adam and Amanda who will pass their knowledge down to Marie and Frank, who in turn can pass it down to Bobby Joe and Jonathan. I can't say how long we

SORCERERS REBORN

may be gone but this shouldn't take more than a week, weather permitting. Any questions?"

No one responded.

"Good, we leave after midnight, there is supposed to be a full moon tonight. Bring only what you think you will need for a one-week trip, ladies."

They ate before leaving, then loaded Susan and Samantha's four-wheel drive truck. Everyone was up to see them off.

Jason figured they could make reasonably good time and he calculated they should be close to the TransCanada Highway's south leg by morning. The route Jason chose, an old forestry road, turned out to be slower than he had expected. There had been a storm south of the Sanctuary that they did not know about until they found the foot of snow on the ground. Even with the use of magic it took them until mid-morning to arrive at their first stop. Susan, Samantha, and Jason ate a much smaller meal than they were used to, not wanting to draw attention to themselves.

Jason checked the charge on the batteries. They were fully charged. As he unplugged the cable, the attendant told him it would be ten dollars for the use of the charger. Jason did not argue because he doubted that a small place like this had much business at this time of year. Jason talked with the gas bar attendant about the back roads.

"They shut down the logging roads before I was born, must be seventy or eighty years ago, but there's some good hunting along those old logging roads, so they're still being used. Those roads go all the way up to the national park up on highway 16 that goes into the BC interior. They may be a little rough in places, but you should be okay with this truck of yours. I'll draw you a rough map."

Soon the three Sorcerers were on a logging road heading north.

"A *little* rough, he said. We are going to have to overhaul the entire suspension when we find this damn place, if we make it that far." Samantha grumbled as she navigated the potholes.

123

It was slow going, but by late afternoon the twins began to sense magic up ahead. The sun was setting when they reached a road going in the right direction. Samantha looked to the east.

"Whatever it is, it's over there somewhere," Samantha said. "We should make camp here and continue in the morning. If our way forward is anything like the road behind us, I for one want to see where I am going."

Jason and Susan didn't argue. They used the earth and rock that was available to form a hut, enlarging the interior to suit their needs—two bedrooms and a common-area. A globe of light in each room gave off enough heat to keep the place comfortable from the chilly night. As they ate, they discussed how they would proceed the next day.

All of them sensed when a creature—no, two creatures—approached their hut.

"Wolves," said Jason. "They probably smelled the food, the meat most likely. If they don't leave by the time we are done eating, we should go out and have a chat with them."

"Isn't that a little risky? After all, they are wild animals," Susan said.

"They are creatures that live in the wild, yes. We are Sorcerers and have our gift to protect us if need be. We have a chance to observe them, SEE them. Let's see if we can change ourselves into wolves. It should be no different from me switching between DeWayne and Jason. The two of you saw how I did that. I am sure the two of you have tried it yourselves, and probably shared that information with the others." When he saw them blush, he knew they knew how.

Susan and Samantha were not convinced, but followed Jason's lead.

The trio stepped outside and saw the wolves standing twenty meters away, silhouetted by the moonlight. They were bigger than Jason expected. From their size he believed they were timber wolves—large, fast, and reportedly, not friendly.

<Hello, my name is Jason, and these are my friends Susan and Samantha. Why are you outside our cave?>

The two wolves looked at him, tilting their heads from side to side, then at each other. A possibly male voice spoke in his head.

<I am Runner, and this is my mate, Luna. You are different from other humans we have encountered, and you do not fear us as they do. We watched you as you made your cave. None of the others we have seen build their caves the way you do. This winter has been hard for us. The snow was deep, and hunting was difficult. We thought we might find some scraps. The others always left scraps behind.>

Jason did not know which one spoke, although he did know that one was male and the other was most likely female. He slowly walked closer, not wanting to spook Runner and his mate. He sat down when he'd covered about half the distance between them, indicating friendship he hoped. Samantha and Susan again followed his lead, but remained on alert.

<My friends and I are Sorcerers. Our beliefs are not the same as other humans. We are creatures of magic and we can do things that the others cannot.>

A large piece of meat appeared in front of each wolf. Jason looked at the twins. He assumed they figured if the wolves had food, they would leave the humans alone.

The wolves jumped back twenty centimeters. Runner spoke. <What is this? Why have you come here to our territory? What things can you do?>

Jason smiled, unsure whether they saw, or even understood, what a smile was.

<My colleagues gave you food, which is a small thing we can do. We are looking for something that is, or was, made with magic. It is not that far from here. We will leave here and look for it when the sun comes up. If you will permit us to cross your territory?>

The two wolves looked at each other. Maybe they were conversing with each other. As Jason waited for a response, he studied the two wolves the same way he had studied himself when he was looking for a new him.

<You can cross, but there is a storm coming. Go back to your cave. We will be close by,> Runner said.

Then each wolf picked up a piece of meat with their strong jaws and ran off into the night. Jason felt the wind getting stronger and looked at his companions. Now that their attention was not on the wolves, they sensed the coming storm.

"What just happened?" Susan asked as they secured the door. "How could we have missed this storm?"

"We were distracted, trying to study our guests instead of paying attention to what was happening around us." Samantha gave Jason a scathing look.

The wind howled most of the night, finally dying down an hour before dawn. Samantha put their dishes and utensils into her backpack. Susan opened the door and snow fell in.

Jason looked out and said, "I don't think we are going anywhere unless we walk. There must be at least two feet of snow out here, and the drifts are probably three or four feet deeper. We will need snowshoes and a couple of walking sticks. We can use wood from the brush over there."

Jason took the lead breaking trail for the twins. They were just getting used to walking with snowshoes when the road ended, the trail to the magic they sought led them uphill. They walked around trees and brush that thinned out as they gained elevation. The snow was not as deep here because it was more open and the wind had blown most of it away, so the snowshoes had to be removed. They stored them in a bush in case they needed them for the return journey. Soon there was nothing but rock all around them. The sun was almost straight overhead, so they found a mostly flat area to rest and eat a cold meal.

"If you look up there to the left, there is a darker line in the rock. That seems to be where we are going." Susan pointed out the anomaly.

The climb wasn't that difficult, and it had warmed up considerably. They found a game trail that seemed to lead straight to where they wanted to go. The trail led to an almost flat, wide shelf with a stream coming from the large split in the rock face. The sun was moving west and would be going down within the next two hours. They decided to wait until morning before investigating any further. They used the loose rock scattered around them to make another cabin.

"Runner and Luna are down there, I can still sense their presence. They appear to be looking for their next meal," Samantha said looking down the slope to the tree line far below.

"It is nice enough out here to have a BBQ. Everything tastes so much better when it is cooked on an open fire." Susan began building a fire pit and grate from the stone.

"We will need some firewood, if you can make enough to cook a meal on, that is?"

Jason imagined a dead fall and it appeared using magic and he set it down a dozen feet from Susan's fire pit. He used magic to section the dead tree into manageable pieces for Susan. The shelf they were on sloped toward the stream, so what was left of the melting snow went in that direction.

Working together, it wasn't long before they were sitting down to eat roast beef and a variety of vegetables. Samantha had made chairs and Jason had created a bubble that covered the shelf—leaving a vent in the top for the smoke to escape—to keep in most of the warmth of the fire. As they ate, Runner and Luna padded through the bubble then sat looking at them.

"I see that the two of you had no trouble running through this snow. I suppose you were teasing us last night when you said hunting was hard because of the deep snow," Susan said.

<You gave us food, didn't you? When winter comes, we are able to move with less trouble than most,> Runner replied.

"How did the hunt go today?" Samantha asked.

<We found a couple of mice. The rabbits we saw can run better in the snow than we can,> Luna said.

"You are welcome to stay here tonight," Jason said. "The wind and cold won't bother you while you are close to us."

Large pieces of meat appeared in front of both wolves.

The Sorcerers studied the wolves as they had the night before. After they retired to their cabin, Jason suggested that the twins watch him change. Samantha wanted to know what would happen to their clothes. He explained to them that when they changed, their clothes changed with them, along with anything else they may be wearing such as a backpack. They practiced changing from their human form into that of a wolf. Once they had changed a half-dozen times they went outside and asked Runner and Luna to observe their progress. Luna told Susan and Samantha that their tails had to be longer and that they would know when they had it right. After a few more tries Susan said, <I see now how your tail helps with balance when you get it right.>

The next morning they put enough of the leftover food to last them the day into their backpacks. They had no idea what they would find, so it was better to be prepared. The rest they left sitting by the grill for the scavengers.

Runner and Luna had left the campsite but were still within the range of their sensory perception.

As Jason removed the bubble he heard a shrill shriek overhead. When he looked up, he saw two eagles diving from the sky at a great speed. They back winged to land by the leftover meat. Jason could sense only hunger, no fear.

Susan and Samantha were pleased at seeing such magnificent creatures this close. The span of their wings was almost two meters, and they stood nearly a meter tall. It was no wonder they had no fear of the three humans standing only a few feet away.

"This is the chance of a lifetime," Samantha said. "We can study them like we did the wolves. Just think of what we could see, and do, if we could fly."

Winter must have been hard for the bald eagles as well, so the three Sorcerers left them to their purloined meal and continued toward the source of the magic.

A short distance on they reached the next plateau, and another hurdle greeted them. Susan cursed, Samantha shook her head, and Jason looked in disbelief at the river of half-frozen water coming from the crevasse.

"Is that where we are going?" Jason pointed toward the fissure.

"Yes, it is, that is where the magic emanates from," Samantha said.

"We have to figure out how we are going to get there from here. Walking is out of the question. Let's return to our cabin and try to figure this out," said Jason.

The eagles were finishing their meal when the Sorcerers returned to camp. Susan didn't want them to leave so she gave a large salmon to each of them.

<What is this?> a male voice asked.

"We can give you all you can eat while we are here. We want to observe you so we can become eagles too."

Susan turned into a wolf long enough for the eagles to see her before she turned back.

<How did you do that?> the male voice asked.

Jason saw an opening. Susan had a great idea. If they were able to turn themselves into these majestic birds, they could fly to whatever was hidden in that crevasse. All he had to do was help Susan convince them to stay long enough to learn.

<I am Jason, and my cohorts are Susan and Samantha. We are Sorcerers on a quest to find a magical object hidden in these mountains. We met a pair of wolves yesterday and studied them until we could change into wolves. We would like to do the same thing with you and your mate.>

<I am Azul, and this is my mate Lima. Our food source has been lacking this winter. Too many hunters like us are hunting the same territory. It will improve as time passes, as others die off. If you want to study us, go ahead. If you keep feeding us we will stay until you leave here.>

By the end of the day the three Sorcerers had managed to master turning into bald eagles. Flying was not so easy though. Jason turned to the two eagles.

"Would you teach us how to fly Azul? It would help us if you shared your knowledge."

Salmon appeared in front of Azul and Lima.

<When the light returns, we will show you,> Azul replied.

The gray dawn of a cold morning found the three Sorcerers following the two birds' instructions on how to fly. The sun was sinking in the west when Azul told them that they would start again in the morning. Jason was too tired to argue.

A good meal followed by a restorative sleep seemed to consolidate their learnings. When they took off the next morning Azul agreed to a flight over the part of the mountain containing the magic. Flying over the gorge, they found a waterfall that created a great deal of mist, which coated the smooth walls of the cavern. They could see that the amount of snow fueling the river cascading into the crevasse was enormous. Even with their enhanced vision they could not see anything more than mist and ice, and Azul warned them not to risk getting ice build-up on their wings.

<Damn it all to hell! We can sense what we are looking for is not that far from the top of the mountain, but we cannot get an exact location. The ice must be interfering in some way,> said Samantha.

<We will continue with our lessons and talk this over when the day is done,> Jason said.

<We believe you are ready to go out on your own. When the light comes again, we will follow, but not interfere.> Lima's sultry voice echoed in their minds.

The Sorcerers spent the evening in their cabin discussing ways to remove the ice, eventually concluding that putting an envelope of hot air over that area could melt the ice. In the morning they tried their theory on a part of wall outside of the crevasse and although the ice was much thinner there it worked as they intended it to.

They put on their backpacks before they changed into eagles and flew into the crevasse, staying well above the mist. Samantha created a bubble-envelope, and the three Sorcerers took turns adding more heat as needed. As the ice melted, an opening in the stone face became visible; an hour later it was completely clear.

<Now what? That hole is too small for us to enter as eagles, and there is no other way for us to get close,> Susan said.

As the Sorcerers' heat dissipated, ice began forming at the bottom of the opening, creating a wide shelf. With a little bit of magical assistance, it became large enough for them to land on. Jason set himself down first, changed into his human form and proceeded into the tunnel. Susan and Samantha followed. Each of them produced a light.

<Let's be careful. Telepathic communication only. We don't know what we are walking into. I will lead; you two stay close behind me,> Jason cautioned.

What they thought was a cave was actually a corridor eight feet wide and ten feet high, with an arched ceiling. The corridor made a wide arc to the right leading them to a large open cavern. Two items covered in dust rested on a podium near the center. A large book sat beside an oval something. Jason reached out and wiped the dust off the oval item and discovered a blue stone with white flecks.

He picked the stone up. It was smooth, and warm considering the cool temperature inside the cavern. Jason placed the stone back on the pedestal and turned his attention to the book. The book looked old, very old. Jason blew most of the dust off. It appeared to be made of leather, with a leather band that connected to latches on both the back and front covers. Raised symbols were visible under the remaining dust on the front cover.

Touching the stone had done nothing, so he reached out and put both hands on the book. As he lifted it off the stand a bright, white light engulfed both him and the book. His eyes opened wide, he pulled the book to his chest, and the light turned to a brilliant blue. Jason's eyes rolled back in his head as he collapsed.

Susan and Samantha watched in shocked silence as the blue light shimmered then vanished as quickly as it had appeared. Jason lay on the floor of the cavern holding the book to his chest.

Samantha knelt by Jason's side and was reaching out to touch him—

<Stop, Sam! We don't know what that book did to Jason, or what it might do to us. I can see he is breathing, let's get him back to our camp and decide what to do from there.>

Samantha nodded. <I think the stone is important too. Do we dare touch it? It didn't do anything to Jason when he touched it.>

Samantha opened her backpack and using telekinesis maneuvered the stone into her backpack. <Right now, I think it's better if we do not take any chances, Sue.>

Susan took a blanket from her pack and spread it on the floor beside Jason. She lifted him up using her magic and placed him in the center of the blanket. They wrapped him up and secured the blanket with rope. By the time they had carried him back to the entrance their energy levels were low. Samantha pulled sandwiches out of her pack.

"How are we going to get him back to the cabin, sis?" Susan asked.

"We do it the same way we got him this far. Once he's levitated, he will be lighter than air so in eagle-form we can carry him."

"I know it isn't that far, but our energy is already low from using our gift repeatedly today. We need to rest first."

When they were ready, they made the ledge wider and longer. They moved Jason to the center, leaving him suspended a foot above the shelf. Samantha elevated herself above him and changed into an eagle. She picked him up in her strong talons and, beating her wings, lifted into the air. Susan was right behind her, connecting minds with her sister to lighten her load. Samantha discovered that carrying a load, regardless of how light it was, made flying more difficult. Something else they had not anticipated.

They were approximately three thousand five hundred meters from the ground. Until they were clear of the mist they had to maintain their height; a fall from that height would not end well.

<I am right below you if you need my help,> Azul told Samantha.

As they flew out of the gorge they descended toward the cabin. With the door opened they used their magic to lift Jason up and move him to his bed.

"I will make a cup of the restorative broth Marie showed us. I think we could use some too. You figure out how we are going to feed it to him, Sue."

When Samantha entered the bedroom, Susan was feeling DeWayne's forehead.

"It's ok Sam, touching him does not transfer whatever spell the book carries to us."

"I don't know if I am willing to touch that book, but it seems safe to touch him. I don't see any physical damage so if I support him, can you feed him that broth Sam?"

Jason responded to the broth almost immediately. He had not eaten since breakfast and they did not know what was going on inside of him. His breathing had become ragged but with the restorative brew it was improving. The book obviously transferred some kind of power to him. They gave him some more of the brew and let him rest.

"He seems to be going through the same thing we did when he first unlocked our powers. I think all we can do right now is to watch over him. He was there for us, now we must repay that gesture."

For the next day they took turns watching over him and feeding him broth. They left the book, still clutched in his hands, resting on his chest. They also looked after the four creatures they had met on their journey, continuing to feed them.

Late that night, Jason began coming out of the book's magically-induced coma. He came around slowly, trying to shake off the drowsy, disoriented feeling. Samantha helped him drink some more broth while Susan made a quick hot meal. As he became more coherent Jason looked at the book still lying on his chest.

"We didn't want to touch it just in case it zapped us too," Samantha said.

She wrapped the book in a towel before lifting it aside to make room for the tray Susan brought. Jason ate the solid food slowly, returning somewhat to his normal self.

Early the next morning Jason told them he was ready to leave and placed the book into his backpack. After a quick breakfast they gathered the rest of their things and stepped out of the building.

Runner, Luna, Azul, and Lima were waiting for them. The Sorcerers thanked them again for their help and left them with food enough for a couple of days. They then returned the plateau back to the way they found it.

The whole trip back home seemed longer than it had going out.

"The three of you look terrible!" Adam said as he reached the truck.

"I'll get some food on the table. We can't wait to hear about your journey," Marie said, smiling.

Jason, Susan, and Samantha took turns regaling them with details of their adventure. Susan and Samantha finally admitted just how scared they had been when Jason was zapped by the book. Jason had to pull it out to show everyone, but nobody else touched it.

"You better let Marie and I check you to make sure there is no internal damage we cannot see," said Frank.

"Did it hurt to change into a wolf?" asked Bobby Jo.

"No, I wasn't sure at first, but I followed my training and slowly changed into a she wolf. When I asked Runner and Luna how I looked, Luna told me my tail was too short, but I would know when I got it exactly right. The tail has a lot to do with their balance you know." Susan obliged them with a demonstration.

This would become one more thing to add to their lessons. As they had learned, being able to change into another creature could be beneficial.

PART 3

THINGS UNEXPECTED

CHAPTER 14

VANCOUVER ISLAND

The men discovered that Jason was the only one who could read the book. They had all picked the book up with no ill effects—but none of them could open it, let alone read it. The women reported the same results when they tried.

Midnight mused on the artifacts. <The book, I have never seen before. The writing is foreign to me, but I believe that stone is a dragon's egg. I have never seen one myself, but I have had them described to me by a real dragon. It was said that Tay'Ron stole one of these eggs some four thousand years ago, and from what I know it was never recovered. Perhaps this is that egg.>

"A dragon's egg! I doubt that will hatch after thousands of years."

<Dragons are creatures of magic. That egg is infused with magic, you said so yourself. Trust me when I say that egg is still viable.>

Midnight narrowed her focus to Jason alone. <Jason can we talk? You have asked me if there are any other secrets I am keeping, and there is one more thing you need to do. There is an island off the west coast that has some magical items I need you to retrieve. I haven't been there for three thousand years so don't expect my memory of the place to be accurate.>

<Midnight, are you talking about Vancouver Island?>

<Yes, I believe it is now called Vancouver Island. It did not have a name when we arrived. When we realized we were no longer on Orighen, and were on an island, we had to find a way off that island. Our search led us to a group native to this world who were fishing just offshore using large boats and nets.

<Before we approached them, the Sorcerers made clothing that looked more like what the people of this world wore. Each Sorcerer bundled their Orighen clothing and weapons in their cloaks to create a secure package, and buried the bundles together in one place. You will need to bring Susan and Samantha, or Amanda and Adam, to help you find the place.

<I chose two creatures to guard the location until it was overgrown. I do not know how the magic might have affected them. It is possible that they are still there. If you think it might help, I can give you images of how I remember the place. Knowing how much things can change over three thousand years, I doubt any image I give you will be useful.>

Jason scratched his friend between the ears. <I suppose we will have to do this the hard way. You go and rest while I talk with the others.>

Once the evening meal had been cleared except for the wine and beer still being sipped, Jason broached the subject of their next quest.

"Our job is to recover those magic objects from Vancouver Island. I would like to ask Frank and Marie if we could use their motorhome for our journey. I figure that there should be at least five of us on this expedition and at least two must have the ability to sense magic from a distance."

Frank frowned. "I don't want to sound conceited, but if our motorhome goes, Marie and I go. It sounds like this may be a dangerous mission. Marie's and my medical training might come in handy."

Adam looked at Susan and Samantha. "Amanda and I would like to go on this quest, but Susan and Samantha have been here the longest, so they have first choice to my way of thinking."

"We will stay behind this time, Adam. You and Amanda are more than capable of detecting these magical artifacts," Samantha said.

"Are there any objections? Then we have our five. We should get some rest and make our plans in the morning," Jason said.

Bobby Joe asked quietly, "Can I go with you? I have never been to Vancouver Island. I know this isn't a sightseeing trip, but I hear that it is quite nice there."

Jason laughed. "I don't see any reason why you can't join us Bobby Joe, so now we are six."

"We have everything organized and the motorhome is stocked and ready to go. The only stops we need to make are to change drivers and charge the batteries. We will leave at first light," Jason said as they finished their evening meal.

"Has everyone remembered their toothbrush?" Marie teased as the explorers climbed into the motorhome.

They laughed and replied in unison. "Yes, Mom."

Frank sat in the driver's seat with Marie as his co-pilot. They waved goodbye to the three Sorcerers who were remaining, and Midnight, as they pulled out of the clearing.

They switched drivers every two hours so the one doing the driving was always fresh. They didn't stop to eat. They had all the makings for meals, and using magic while concealed in the motorhome was not going to be seen by anyone. Because they didn't keep regular hours, food was always ready in the motor home's kitchen. It was evening when they arrived at the ferry terminal. They had time to stretch their legs before catching the last ferry going to Victoria, the city on the southernmost tip of Vancouver Island.

Frank and Marie had lived there before and knew of a campsite a few miles north of the city. The decision to stop for the night was unanimous. After a good meal and a solid night's sleep, they continued their journey.

Midnight had told them that the place they were looking for was next to a mountain range, so they chose the inland highway. Bobby Joe drove, leaving the others free to survey the land west of the highway where the mountain range was. Because they were traveling at a slower speed, they did not cover much distance by the end of the day. There were turnoffs to every small town along the coast.

They took the next turnoff. They found a motel that had stalls and chargers for motorhomes. They had supper before taking a walk down to the shoreline. They watched a cruise ship, which Marie told them was probably going to Alaska, as they walked along the beach.

"That ship is huge! I have never been to the ocean before. Are they all like that?" Bobby Joe asked.

"That's one of the largest I have seen," Marie told her. "They seem to get larger every year."

As they walked back to the motorhome, Adam stopped and turned to the south east looking up to the sky. "Do any of you feel that?"

They followed his line of sight.

"I don't see anything, but I sense something that is, or contains magic coming our way. It is getting closer by the second," Amanda said.

"I feel it too," Marie added.

It took a full minute before what looked like a star became visible, and it was obvious that it was getting larger by the second as it rushed toward them.

"It appears to be slowing down, and I think it's coming our way. Maybe we should run," Adam said.

Jason could not sense any magic, but he had seen hundreds of meteors in his days and this one was different. It did appear to be slowing down, and that was disturbing. They watched as it came closer, and it seemed to be heading right for them. Then it made a bit of an adjustment, curving a bit toward the mountains before straightening out like it knew where it was going. When it went over them it seemed to be only a few hundred meters in the air.

The bulk was bright orange with streaks of yellow, and the tail was a brilliant blue. When it landed, they saw a bright yellow burst of light, and then it faded to nothing.

"That was awesome, and a bit scary at the same time," Amanda said.

Jason turned to them. "That is the strangest meteor I have ever seen. We need to get to it before anybody else does. Whatever magic it contains, we have to retrieve it."

They returned to the motorhome and drove up to the inland highway. Jason drove so that Adam and Amanda, and Frank and Marie, could link minds with their respective partners in order to expand the reach of their senses to find anything that possessed magic. Bobby Joe sat up front with Jason. He didn't want to drive too fast in case they missed their original target, the reason for the quest. If they found that first, they would have to mark the spot, and continue until they found the meteor.

This could be a very long night.

Three hours later Amanda told them that she could sense something up ahead and the other three echoed her enthusiasm. Jason slowed even more. They drove for another half an hour, one of the searchers giving Jason updates every couple of minutes.

"We are really close," Amanda said.

Jason kept his speed the same. There was no indication that anyone else was out looking for the meteor.

"STOP!" Marie and Amanda shouted at the same time.

Jason stopped.

"We are right beside it, whichever one it is. We will have to check it out before going any further. It is that way." Adam pointed to the mountains to the west.

"We can't park here. We need to keep driving until we find someplace a little more secluded."

"Up ahead, that looks like a sign. Why don't we see what it says?" Bobby Joe pointed to a triangular object up the road, which was reflecting the light from the motorhome's headlights. It read, ROADSIDE PULL OUT, with an arrow beneath pointing west. Jason pulled into the driveway and followed the short road to the rest stop.

"What's that over there, is that a road or a trail maybe?" Bobby Joe pointed to an opening in the trees at the back of the clearing.

Jason backed up and turned the motorhome in the direction Bobby Joe had indicated. They stepped out and checked the narrow road. The trees provided a canopy blocking out the moonlight, so Jason sent a light into the darkness. There were two ruts leading into that darkness, the ground in between them slightly overgrown.

Frank shrugged. "We go as far as we can. If we can't turn around, we back out—I can do that. This way, we will not be seen from the road. Okay, let's do this, time's wasting away."

Frank drove, going as fast as the pothole-riddled road would allow, which was slower than walking. The road went in quite far before the head lights showed it widening into a kind of cul-de-sac at the end. Frank turned the motorhome to the south and stopped ten feet from the trees.

"Do we leave someone here to babysit the motorhome, or do we all go?" Jason asked.

"I think the motorhome can take care of itself, Jason," Frank said.

It was agreed that they would all go. There was no knowing what they would find, and the motorhome was hidden. Frank waited until the others had a dim light before turning the motorhome's engine off. The trees were rain forest high and several feet apart, which made walking easier. They came to a meadow and Jason stopped them just inside the tree line. The earth was pushed up on the far side of the meadow, closer to the mountain.

<We will use telepathy from here on until we see what there is to see,> Jason said. <That whitish lump by the crater—it's a strange looking rock.>

Jason looked at the others for confirmation that they understood before motioning them forward. As they stepped onto the grass of the meadow, the rock moved. A portion seemed to break off the larger section. Bobby Joe cautiously walked forward, changing into a wolf as she did.

<The smaller one is a wolf, the larger one looks like a bear. They both have the gift.> Bobby Joe opened her broadcast to include the animals. <We mean you no harm. Come here and sit with us. We will talk wolf to wolf.>

The bear slowed and the wolf stopped. An unusual pair, they were natural enemies at any other time. Jason studied the bear. He had studied another bear in a zoo not long after he had received his gift and this one was the same kind, only much older. Not that one grizzly bear would be very different from another.

<As my friend said we mean you no harm. We would like to see the meteor if you will let us? That ball of fire, the one that fell from the sky a short time ago,> Jason asked.

<We are the guardians, and we must stop anyone from taking the treasure.> A deep voice reverberated in their minds.

The bear was on all four legs, his lips parted with his sharp teeth showing, looking like he was ready to attack.

Bobby Joe sat and, showing no fear, looked at both the wolf and the bear as she spoke.

<Do you remember the cat called Midnight? She sent us here to retrieve the treasure. We are Sorcerers, much as she is, and you

and your bear friend are Sorcerers as well. She would have come herself, but she is ill and is unable to travel.>

A female voice answered. <We have dealt with humans before, they are deceitful. Why should we trust you?>

<Did those other humans change into a wolf right before your eyes? You and the bear are Sorcerers like us, so you must be able to sense that we are not trying to deceive you?>

<She speaks truly lupus. I do not believe they lie. Maybe they can help the others?> The bear's head bobbed up and down.

<I don't understand 'the others.' Who are these others, where are these others?> Bobby Joe asked.

<They fell from the sky. They are over there in the hole.> The wolf admitted turning her head and looking toward the divot at the far side of the meadow.

<Marie, Frank, go see what she's talking about,> Jason asked the two doctors.

Frank looked into the crater, which was only three or four feet deep. <Oh my god, there are two women in here!>

<Amanda, Bobby Joe, come here and put some clothes on these two, they must be half-frozen by now,> Marie added.

Frank and Marie checked the two women while Amanda and Bobby Joe dressed them in warm clothing and covered them with blankets.

<We need a couple of stretchers to bring these two back to the motorhome. They will need food and warmth as soon as possible.> Frank jumped out of the crater and motioned for Jason and Adam to help him.

The bear and the wolf sat by the crater watching as Marie continued examining the two women. The men fashioned poles for two stretchers from the limbs of a dead tree then used magic to weave grass together to join the two poles completing the stretchers. They lifted the two women out of the crater and loaded them onto the stretchers. When Jason looked at the woman with the lighter red hair an unusual feeling surged through his body, emotions he had not felt since his wife died over fifty years ago.

<Bobby Joe and I will stay here with our new friends,> Jason said. <Perhaps we can show them how to change forms. That might take some time, and some smooth talking.>

Marie and Frank picked up one of the stretchers, assisted by their magic, while Adam and Amanda picked up the other.

<Amanda and I will come back when these two are safe and warm in the motorhome,> Adam said as the four of them headed back to the vehicle.

<I will follow your lead,> Bobby Joe said to Jason.

Jason looked at the bear and the wolf.

<You say that you are the guardians. Not for the two women who were here, because they just arrived. What is it you are guarding? The treasure Midnight requested that you guard, I think. If you let us take this treasure, we will still need your services as guardians until we can turn the treasure over to Midnight.>

The bear looked at the wolf. If they were communicating, they were doing it between themselves.

<We cannot come with you as we are. The other humans would try to kill us. We are, after all, considered wild animals,> the female voice said.

<Remember how I changed into a wolf?> Bobby Joe asked. <We are Sorcerers and the two of you are Sorcerers. Jason and I can show you how to change into the human form if you would like, the choice is yours to make. I will say this though, both of you have already lived thousands of years, and you will continue to live for thousands more. Wouldn't it be a better life living with us? Think about it, talk it over together.>

The wolf and the bear walked a short distance away. Jason and Bobby Joe waited patiently, watching the two snow-white creatures.

The bear turned and walked back to them, the wolf by his side.

<Show us how this changing thing works?>

<We will move apart to give us some privacy. The fewer the distractions the better it is for everyone,> Jason said.

Bobby Joe touched the wolf on the forehead. The wolf flinched at the touch and then regained her composure.

<I will remove my outer clothing so you can see just my human form, then change back into a wolf. You can watch how I change back to human and learn. I have showed you that you need to look at every part of me, every detail. Like you, if my tail is too short then my balance is off. To be a human, you want to get everything right as well.>

The wolf watched Bobby Joe as she slowly changed from wolf to human and back again several times before she tried it herself. The human-wolf was beautiful, with long silver hair reaching almost to her waist. She was well proportioned, slim...and completely naked. She had some similarities to Bobby Joe, the eyes turned up slightly at the corners. Bobby Joe slipped on her own clothes then helped the naked woman with her clothing, conjuring garments that were loose fitting and easy to move around in. When they were done, Bobby Joe conjured a mirror and let the human-wolf see herself.

Jason was having the same conversation with the bear. When he changed into a bear, the bear sat down and looked at him. Jason asked the bear to watch him change back. Jason slowly changed back into his human form. He did this several times before the bear was able to mimic what Jason was doing and the bear changed into his human form. He too had waist length silver hair.

Jason used his ability to see that the human-bear had it right, and conjured loose fitting clothing.

<You have done well, my friend. Let me give you your first lesson.>

Jason touched the human-bear on the forehead, giving him the knowledge of human speech, just as Bobby Joe was doing for the human-wolf.

Jason and Bobby Joe steadied the new humans as they began to walk. They were used to walking on four legs and now they only had two. Adam and Amanda came into the clearing and stopped to watch the proceedings on the meadow.

<Our new friends are going to need names,> Amanda said after hearing them being referred to as 'wolf' and 'bear.'

<Maybe, for now at least, we could call our new bear friend Brian, and our new wolf friend, Louise. Of course, if they would like to change them later, they can.>

Jason looked at her, then at the newly changed bear and wolf.

<The choice is yours. If you like your new names then we will use them, if not, we will let you choose later.>

<Brian sounds like a good name,> the bear said.

<Louise sounds like a good name for now,> the wolf agreed.

Brian showed them where the treasure was and they dug it up, removing six bundles wrapped in hooded cloaks. Jason was surprised at how well preserved they were. Jason and Adam each took two of the bundles and Bobby Joe and Amanda each took one. They raised them off the ground using magic and walked back to the motorhome, with Brian and Louise in between them.

When they arrived at the motorhome, they piled the bundles outside and took Brian and Louise in to meet Frank and Marie. It was a bit crowded, but they would make do. Marie came out of the back bedroom.

"We can't find anything wrong with our two patients. There are no external injuries of any kind, and I can't sense any internal ones either. Frank and I gave them some broth, but there's no change so far. Either Frank or I should always be with them. Who are our new guests?"

"Marie, meet Brian and Louise, formerly known as bear and wolf, guardians of the treasure. We will begin teaching them as we travel. We are ok to travel, aren't we?" Bobby Joe looked at Marie inquiringly.

"I don't think travel will be a problem. I believe the sooner we are home the better. We do have everything we came for plus a few extras, don't we? Would you like Frank and me to check our new friends?"

Jason smiled. "I think they are ok Marie, and your suggestion that you and Frank continue to look after our two alien friends is their best chance of survival. Leave the driving to the rest of us."

CHAPTER 15

EXTRATERRESTRIALS

After Jason and Adam loaded and secured the bundles on the rack on top of the motorhome, they left the island by way of the ferry from Nanaimo, since it was closest. During the day and a half trip back to the Sanctuary the two newcomers remained in a comatose state.

Brian and Louise, on the other hand, were very much alive and eager to learn. As bear and wolf, guardians for almost three thousand years, they had become close friends. Now that they were both human it was clear that they had strong feelings for each other.

When they arrived at the Sanctuary, Samantha, Susan, and Johnathan were there to greet them, but Midnight was nowhere to be seen. Jason asked where she was but no one could say. *She will show up when she shows up,* he thought.

After the patients were settled into a room, Marie went downstairs to get something to eat for Frank and herself, and to give a quick report. "They are improving, but we believe they are far from coming around at this time. We will have to wait and see."

She pushed the food cart into the dumb waiter and went back upstairs.

Midnight had told them earlier that what they had first believed to be a rock was more likely to be a dragon's egg and it would still hatch. Those not caring for their two guests took turns holding the dragon's egg, simulating motherly love. Everyone hoped that it would hatch. There were people coming from another world, strange books of magic, so why not have a real dragon too?

That night, Marie's mental voice alerted the others that their guests had awakened, and that she and Frank could use some help. The women were quite upset to find that they were not where they should be.

Marie said they were quite vocal, asking, "Who are you and where are we?"

When Jason entered the common room from his bedroom, he put the egg back on its pedestal. Marie was there with the others.

"They are weak," Marie said, "and they need real food, but they keep insisting that we return them to some palace in Geldania. Apparently one of them is the queen. They are from Geldania because we can understand them. They are in shock, so they are not willing to listen to reason, and they keep calling Frank one of them, and I have no idea what they are talking about."

Jason digested what Marie had told them. "Susan and Samantha, would you go upstairs with Marie and see if you can get them to drink some wine maybe. Use your gift to make the glasses and the wine right there in front of them. Maybe if they see that you are Sorcerers too, they might calm down a bit."

Samantha, Susan, and Marie went back upstairs.

"We have to find out how they got here," Jason said shaking his head as he walked into the kitchen to prepare a meal for their guests.

From what Marie said, they think we had something to do with it. She mentioned a palace and Geldania. Could they really be Queen Jakiera, and her sister Tarisha? I suppose that is a possibility. They would be a target for anyone trying to take over the country again.

The southern Sorcerers I imagine. It is paramount that we gain their trust if they are who I think they are.

Frank stood at the end of the bed. The two ladies, blankets pulled up under their chins, sat side by side glaring at him. Marie looked at Frank, and using telepathy asked him to leave. Frank didn't argue with her.

Samantha and Susan took his place at the end of the bed.

"Food is being brought up for you. Would you like some wine or another beverage while you wait for the food?" Susan said in Geldanian. Her tone told the two guests that she would take no nonsense from them.

Samantha moved to the side of the bed where the strawberry-blonde woman lay. She conjured a glass and watched as it filled with wine. Samantha took a sip from the glass to show them that it wasn't poison, and then handed it to the woman.

"It's wine. You can drink it or not, but you must be thirsty by now."

Susan did the same thing for the red-haired woman. They both took tentative sips before drinking deeply. A knock at the door signaled the food had arrived. Marie opened the door and took the cart from Amanda and the wine jug from Louise. The platters were on raised trays that fit over the hips and sat firmly on the bed.

"You should eat slowly. You don't want to bring up what you eat because it won't do you much good if you throw it up all over the bed, and I am not in the mood to clean it up. I am a healer as is my husband and we are doing everything we can to keep you alive and find out what happened to you," Marie said.

They were leery of the food at first, and the three women that had given it to them, but the smell of the food won over their mistrust. They savored the food and wine once they began to eat. They realized how weak they were after eating and told Marie they needed to rest.

"My sister and I will stay with you just in case you need anything," Samantha said with a smile.

Marie took the cart back downstairs and reported to the others.

"If they do not trust men, I think it would be better if the women looked after them. For now, at least," Jason said as he picked up the book and the egg, and went toward his apartment on the main floor. "Make sure they know that there are men here as well, and that all of us living here will not let any harm come to them while they are under our care. They have to trust us, all of us."

"Once they rest and have some more food maybe they will be more inclined to listen to the truth," Susan mused quietly in English. "Of course, if I was in their shoes I would probably be just as frightened as they are."

"Marie told us that one of them said she was a queen. Jason suggested they may be Jakiera and Tarisha from our dreams. Should we try calling them by those names, see what kind of response we get? If that proves to be true, then why are they here?"

When the two women woke up, they were not as troubled as they had been earlier. Samantha gave them each a glass of wine and asked them if they would like some more food. The two women said yes to the offer.

Susan went downstairs and with Bobby Joe's help put together a meal for their two guests. When they entered the room the one with the lighter red hair frowned looking at Bobby Joe. Speaking in the language of Geldania the red-haired woman said, "Are you all women here, other than the male healer?"

"There are six women and five men living here. We all have the gift of sorcery. Do you remember a Furl Cat named Midnight?" Bobby Joe asked. "Although she has had to change her appearance on this world due to health reasons and to fit in, she is still the same cat. Perhaps I can ask her to come up here to visit with you."

Both women looked at her then at the others.

"Midnight was lost in the last battle, along with six of our friends. You tell more lies. I was there and I saw them as they were disintegrated into nothing by Tay'Ron." The red-haired woman's voice broke as she spoke.

"You say you saw them being disintegrated, but they were not. Tay'Ron sent them here, to this world. He also infected them with a slow acting virus that eventually took the lives of your friends. They looked for a cure, and a way to get back home, but found nothing to aid them in either matter. Midnight is a creature of magic and can take the gift from someone who is dying into herself.

"As the others died Midnight took their gift into her, and maybe, that gave her the ability to live a much longer life," Susan said. "She was also infected and over the past ten years it has taken its toll on her as well. She is dying now, and she chose us to give your friends' gifts to. We have all accepted that. We can only try to help you find a way back home to Geldania, if that is posable."

"Before we share any more information with you, I would like to introduce those of us who are here now. I am Susan, this is my sister Samantha, and this is Bobby Joe. You already met Marie and Frank, our healers. You are both Sorcerers as well and we will do what we can to keep you safe while you remain here."

The lighter haired one tried to get out of the bed but found she was much weaker than she thought she was. Samantha caught her before she fell to the floor and helped her to get back in bed. When she caught her breath, she said, "I am Jakiera and this is my sister Tarisha. If what you say is true, then we have to try and work together."

The red-haired woman, Tarisha, was not so forgiving. Marie stepped up to the side of the bed.

"How do we know you're telling the truth?" Tarisha said. "Can you prove to us that what you say is truth and not lies?"

"We can prove everything we have told you," Marie said. "When the two of you have healed from the abuse you were put through coming to this world, we will show you that you are no longer on your world. Some manners from both of you would go a long way. Do you want some more to eat or are you going to rest first?"

Tarisha started to say something but Jakiera stopped her.

"My sister can be overprotective sometimes. I think we should rest for a while."

Bobby Joe chuckled to herself as she pushed the cart out the door and down the hall to the dumb waiter. Susan and Samantha joined her as she walked downstairs. "Marie has a way of being both firm and taking the sting out her scolding in the same breath." Susan smiled as they entered the kitchen. Jakiera and Tarisha had been through more than she, or most of the others could understand.

⸻ ∘oo∙❊∙oo∘ ⸻

While Marie, Samantha, Susan, and Bobby Joe were looking after their guests Jason suggested it was time to see what treasure they had found. He asked Adam to gather the remaining Sorcerers and meet him in the barn.

"There you are, John," Adam said. "Jason wants you to come out to the barn with the rest of us. We are going to open those bundles."

John closed the laptop he was using and put the dragon's egg back on its pedestal. The Sorcerers walked to the barn where six tables, each with a bundle, had been set up.

"Let's each take a table, or you can pair up and take a table. It's time to open these and see what kind of treasure we have. After all these bundles are the reason we went on that quest to begin with," said Jason.

Adam walked up to one table. John and Frank took the next two. Jason the fourth. Brian and Louise took the next table and Amanda took the last one. They removed the straps that bound each bundle and opened the cloaks that served as wrappings. In addition to the clothing that was worn by the individual, each bundle had two swords in their scabbards and the belts they attached to, along with waist belts with various knives attached. Some also had an assortment of throwing knives.

Each of the bundles had two leather pouches, one of which contained jewelry, the other, coins made from gold and silver. The money was not from Earth. The only thing that was missing was footwear. Jason picked up a sword and pulled it partway from its sheath then slid it back in.

"Once Jacky and Tara are well enough to come out here, maybe they can identify the owners of each bundle," Jason said. "Let's keep everything as it is for now."

"Jacky and Tara? You're going to give them nicknames before you even meet them?" Adam asked.

"I do not think they will mind. From the dreams we all have, two women from Geldania have the same names. It is possible that these two women are the same ones," Jason replied.

They left the barn and returned to the house. Marie and Bobby Joe were fixing another meal for the two guests. Midnight was still nowhere to be found. Bobby Joe picked up one of the laptops as they passed through the common room. "You told them we would prove to them that they are no longer on Orighen. I believe this will do that and put a stop to any more arguments."

Marie nodded. "Tarisha is not going to like this, Bobby Joe." Marie put the cart into the dumb waiter and the two of them went upstairs.

After Jakiera and Tarisha finished their meal Bobby Joe took the laptop and crawled up onto the bed between the two sisters. She opened the laptop, which tuned it on.

Tarisha frowned and Jakiera's eyes narrowed.

"What kind of magic it this?" Tarisha asked.

"This is technology," Bobby Joe said. "This will show you that you are not on Orighen anymore."

She showed them pictures of the Earth. Pictures of tall skyscrapers, large cities, vistas, and the moon. They saw cars, trucks, and many other vehicles traveling on four and five lane highways. As they looked at the pictures the color drained from their faces.

"I think we should rest for a while. Tarisha and I have a lot to talk about, alone," Jakiera said.

Marie and Bobby Joe exchanged a glance. Bobby Joe slid off the bed and helped Marie gather the empty dishes. As they left the room an invisible Midnight entered.

When they were alone, Jakiera said, "Tara there will be no more argument from you. Whoever did this to us is most likely in charge of the palace right now. We have never heard of traveling on our world let alone between worlds. These people are our only hope if we are going to survive here."

"This is hard for me to accept, Jacky. This can only be the work of the southern Sorcerers, and that means they found a way into the palace, and that means that someone in the palace is working with them. From what I remember there must be at least thirteen southern Sorcerers to pull something of this magnitude off." Tara said, her face showing her disapproval.

"Perhaps it does, Tara. We cannot dwell on that right now. This is not Orighen and we have no way of getting back there, for now. The women who have been taking care of us are all Sorcerers and they say that the men are, too. We join them, become part of their family so to speak. I would like to talk with this Midnight; get the facts straight from the cat's mouth."

"You have doubts too I see. They are kind, and the food is very good. I will not stop thinking of our home, Jacky, regardless of our situation. Maybe we can learn from them, and maybe we can teach them things they don't know. Right now, we need to regain our strength. Whatever method was used to send us here has taken its toll on us, Jacky, and if that happens every time one does this traveling spell or whatever sent us here, I do not want to go through it again."

Jacky smiled at her. "If you want to get home again, you're going to have to deal with it at least one more time, Tara. We both will. The only good thing is that we already know what to expect." She laughed at the irony of her words.

They felt something jump up onto the bed. A black cat appeared, sitting at the end of the bed.

<You know who I am Queen of Geldania. I have been invisible to the others since you arrived trying to figure out how this could have happened again. We believed that Tay'Ron was dead. Even as weak as I am, I saw and felt you coming here. Of course, I did not know it was you and your sister but when I felt the magic the other day, I believed he had sent someone else here. When I saw the two of you, I was sure of my suspicions.>

"Tay'Ron is dead. One of his minions must have found whatever Tay'Ron used to send you here and used it to send us here as well. So you have been avoiding us because…"

<I am told they found you naked, but I thought you might know how to get me back home. I have since realized that you did not chose to come here on your own.>

"There was a report of an unknown ship sighted to the east. Tara went to investigate. If it was the beginning of another attempt by the southern Sorcerers to invade our lands, we had to be on top of it this time. It turned out to be nothing. You know how hot it can get in Geldania, so when Tara and I finished going over her notes we went to bed, naked, as is common when it is so hot. We woke up here and you know what has happened since we arrived. If what we suspect is true, then Geldania is probably overrun by southerners as we speak."

<That may be, but there is nothing you can do about that. I have been trying to return to Orighen for over three thousand years, there is no way back. For now, you have to recover and get used to the fact that you may never see Geldania again.>

Midnight left them.

Jacky and Tara talked until they grew too tired and fell asleep.

Jason looked at Marie and Bobby Joe as they came down the stairs. "How are they doing?"

"We have confirmed that they are indeed Tara and Jacky from our dreams. They need some time to discuss things. They didn't want to believe our story, but there can be no doubt in their minds now," Marie said as she retrieved the cart from the dumb waiter.

"I suppose, if I were to wake up in a strange place, with people I didn't know, on another world altogether, I would doubt them too. I will go up and talk to them later, after they have rested," said Bobby Joe as she put the laptop away.

Jason nodded. "You did the right thing. However, I think it is time they met the rest of the household. You and the others have been doing everything so far. It's time for the men to do our part."

"Well, in all fairness, you have taken over the barn chores while we've been playing nursemaids," Marie said with a smile.

Jason, John, and Frank loaded a cart with two trays of food and drink and put it in the dumb waiter. Frank knocked on the door and announced that they had food for them. One of the women told them to come in.

Frank entered the room first, with Jason backing in pulling the cart while John pushed. When Jason turned around, both women gasped and stared at him.

Jakiera took a deep breath. "You look a lot like someone we knew a very long time ago. We are sorry for our reaction, but we were not expecting to see someone who looks so much like an old friend."

"There is no need for apologies," Jason said. "Midnight gave me Richard's magic, and that may have influenced my choice of visage when I needed to create this persona."

He brought a tray around the end of the bed to Jakiera. As she took it, she felt the emotions she once knew rise up inside her like a surge of flood water. A love that was never consummated, the feeling of that loss, and now, he was right here in front of her. She knew this was not Richard, and she tried unsuccessfully to quash the rising tide of her emotions. When she became queen, Richard and she decided that they both had their part to do when it came to the war against Tay'Ron. It was a hard choice, but they agreed to wait until the war was over to begin the relationship they both wanted. Neither could have known that the war would last as long as it did and how it would end.

"The women of the house have been working very hard to help you heal and get mobile. It's time we men did our part. When you are finished with your meal we will see if you are ready to walk around some more," John said with his most charming smile.

Jason removed the tray from in front of Jakiera, and John removed Tarisha's once they were finished.

"I would like you two to get up and try walking around your bed, for a few minutes anyway." Frank put on his best bedside manner.

The two were unsteady on their feet and needed support from Jason and John. Frank watched the women closely. The journey from Geldania must have used up most of their energy. Frank decided not to let them overdo it for now, as that might make things worse.

When Jakiera and Tarisha returned to their bed, Frank checked their vital signs.

"I will have some exercise equipment brought up here, so you can do some gentle exercising while you're in bed. That should help you rebuild the muscle loss from your journey and help give you back your strength. You should rest now. Rest, exercise, and food will help you recover."

When the men were gone, Tara looked at her sister. "I saw that look on your face Jacky. He is not Richard. I know you have not found another love like the two of you had so long ago, but to find it again on a world we know nothing about? I was just as shocked as you were. However, on a second look this Jason is not

Richard, even if he carries his magic. There are similarities, but there are also obvious differences."

"Would you deny me the chance at having real love again Tara? As you said, I have met no one who made me feel this way since I saw him before the final battle. To think that being sent to this world, by southern Sorcerers I presume, I would find a man who might be the man I have been searching for all my life. I saw in his eyes that he longs for me as well, Tara. Tell me you did not see that too."

Tara shook her head. "I am only looking out for you Jacky. If they find a way to get us home, then you are going to get your heart broken again. Do you think he will leave his world and come to ours? Or are you going to stay here with him? These are the choices that you will have if they find a way to send us back to Geldania."

"I will decide what is in my best interest Tara. I am not the Queen of Geldania while I am here on this world, and you are not the admiral of my army. We are just Tara and Jacky here. If they cannot find a way to get us home, then we are both here until the end of time. Are we not?"

"Lots of good food, plenty of exercise and they should be mostly back to normal," Marie was saying in the common room. "Of course, I do not know what normal is for them, but they are definitely human, so I would say a week, give or take a few days."

Both Brian and Louise had a laptop open on the table in front of them, learning about society. What was acceptable according to the dictates of humanity, and what was not? They had been told what they read about the rules were just guidelines. For a man and woman who used to be a bear and a wolf, they were doing quite well. Midnight had given them longevity, so they would be able to last long enough for the grass and trees to grow over the place where those bundles had been buried. She didn't count on the magic from what they left behind seeping into the earth surrounding the site, and into the ones she chose as her guardians.

Two different kinds of magic coming together over hundreds of years turned the pair into what they were today just as it had with the gifts of her long-lost friends.

Brian and Louise were eager to learn. They spoke the English language well and were learning the language of Orighen as well. When it came to their lessons using magic, they were progressing much faster than the others did when they first started. Brian, like Jason, had taken an interest in the great battles from Earth's past. He especially paid attention to the planning, and strategies, of those in charge of those battles. He studied the way each general moved his troops, how they tried to outthink their opponent. Louise was fascinated with medicine and medical procedures. She spent time with both Marie and Frank, learning everything she could from them.

Jason knew that they would be an essential part of their family at the Sanctuary. He gave them the same attention as he did any of the others. Right now, his mind was on the two from another world. He felt like he should know them better than he did.

CHAPTER 16

A NEW LIFE

Frank and Jason went out to the barn and collected two sets of gear, which they placed close by Tara and Jacky's bed for easy access. Jason explained how to use each item and Frank stressed the fact that they had to be careful not to overdo it, or they might set their recovery back days or even weeks.

"Marie and Louise will see that you get out of bed and walk around for a while each day. Please do not try and overdo that either. Marie is the best healer here and I've worked with her a long time. Believe me when I say she will watch both of you closely. We are here to help you, but that means you have to do your part to help yourselves." Frank's voice was firm as he gave his patients their prescription.

"In the dreams that came with our gifts we knew you as Jacky and Tara. Is there going to be a problem if we use these names for you?" Jason asked.

"Tara and Jacky will be fine. They are the names we have been called since we were children," Tara answered.

"I am certain our dreams are a form of your old friends' memories, as we each see the same things but from different perspectives. However, we are not the people who possessed the gifts before us."

Every time Jason looked at Jacky, he had that feeling of a love lost, renewed. He did not know what to do about it though. Jacky was from another world, and if he was able to find a way to send them back to their own world, he would be left alone again. That was one of the reasons he had been alone for the past fifty-some years. Why was falling in love so damn complicated? He tried to push the thoughts out, but they were not going anywhere.

Over the next month, Jacky and Tara improved daily. Louise enjoyed working with the two doctors, preparing high-protein meals with a full measure of vitamins, and caring for the patients. For the first couple of days the three healers took Tara and Jacky for short walks, up and down the upstairs hallway, guiding and supporting them until the two sisters were able to walk on their own with the aid of walking canes. By the end of the week they could navigate the stairs and Marie suggested moving the exercise routine outside.

Jason was sitting in a chair with the book on his lap and the egg tucked in between his legs when Tara, Jacky, Susan, and Samantha came downstairs intending to walk out to the barn. Jacky stopped to ask Jason what he was reading.

"This is a book we found hidden in the mountains to the west of here. Midnight believes it is a book from a world other than Earth or Orighen. It mostly deals with magic. I am hoping that it might have the spell that will get you home."

"You think it might contain the secrets we need?"

"It is possible that it might, but it is also possible that it might not."

A loud ping interrupted the conversation. Jason set the book on the table beside the chair and looked between his legs. The egg had hairline fractures radiating from a central point near one end. A second later the egg exploded, throwing fragments of shell in every direction. Jason and the four women threw their hands up to protect themselves from the fragments.

Sky-blue legs and a long tail were visible. The rest of the shell was pushed away with force and landed on the floor a few feet away. A light-blue lizard-like creature about ten inches long with small wings just below the shoulders of its front legs, a long neck, and a head shaped like an elongated triangle, now sat between Jason's legs.

The creature looked up and saw Jason. Its head twisted to one side and it let out a squawk.

<Get me some raw meat cut into small pieces and maybe some milk. What in hell does a newborn dragon eat anyway?>

Samantha ran into the kitchen and grabbed a bowl. Using the gift, she filled it with small pieces of meat. She took out another and filled it halfway with milk and placed both on a tray.

Samantha handed Jason the bowl of meat. The little creature looked at him as he offered the bowl to the newborn. It sniffed the contents then took a piece of meat, then lifted its head and swallowed it whole.

When the little one had emptied both bowls it curled up in Jason's lap and promptly went to sleep.

<Can someone tell me what in hell I am supposed to do now?> Jason asked of no one in particular.

Jacky looked at Jason, then at Susan and Samantha. "What's going on?"

Susan shushed her and motioned them into the kitchen. "Do you not know how to speak telepathically? We were talking mentally so we didn't scare the newborn."

"We didn't hear you talking! We do know how to talk mentally and used to use it often. It doesn't seem to be working on your world though," said Tara.

Susan looked at her. "We are going to have to work on that. We don't know anything about what happened to the two of you on, or because of, this journey of yours. It has taken you a week to get your physical strength back, maybe it takes longer for your gift to recover."

Tara looked at Susan and then at Jacky. "We haven't tried using magic. Do you think it is possible that we can't use it anymore?"

"Both of you have the gift; we can all feel it. Maybe you should give yourselves a little more time to recover. Let's not worry about it for now. I am sure we can get you through this."

Samantha prepared two more bowls of meat for later and put them in the fridge. She wondered if that was what they should be feeding this newborn dragon. Maybe Frank and Marie would have an answer?

Frank looked at the others in the barn. "What do you think that was all about? Get me some raw meat, and milk, and something about a newborn dragon. Has our egg hatched?"

Frank, Marie, Louise, and Brian left the barn and walked toward the house. They met Adam, Amanda, John, and Bobby Joe coming out of the greenhouse, each carrying a basket of fruits or vegetables.

"We should see what's going on in there," Adam said grinning. "It sounds like that dragon egg might have hatched. If it has, we have a new family member."

Jason looked at the small creature in his lap. The whole household gathered around him.

<We have a new life in the house, I see,> Amanda said.

<It really is a dragon! What are we going to name it? Him? Her?> asked Bobby Joe.

<Can you pick that little one up and hold it in your arms Jason?> Marie asked.

Jason carefully gathered the dragon into his hands and got up from the chair, moving slowly. As he did Marie took the throw from the chair and a cushion from one of the couches and made a nest-like bed in front of the fireplace. She indicated to Jason to put his charge in it.

<It knows your smell and the throw from your chair will smell like you. It will help to keep the little one calm,> Marie said.

Jason placed the baby dragon in the nest. The dragon babe adjusted itself and continued sleeping.

<This one does need a name, but we don't even know if it is male or female,> Jason said. <We can, however, put together a list of male and female names that you think would be suitable for a dragon to choose from. That way everyone has a say in the little one's future.>

Frank noticed that Samantha was whispering to Tara and Jacky and raised his eyebrow at her.

"Jacky and Tara are currently unable to hear our mental conversations, so I was relaying the gist of our conversations to them." Samantha spoke out loud before adding mentally, <Actually, could you and Marie come into the kitchen so we can chat?>

When the baby dragon woke from its nap, it caused a fuss.

"Maybe it needs its diaper changed," John said.

Jason looked at him, shaking his head. "You might want to see if you can figure out how we will use said diaper on this little one. I think it is probably hungry again."

Jason took the newborn to the kitchen and placed it on the table. He placed one of the bowls of meat and a bowl of milk in front of the dragon. Then he added a bowl of mixed vegetables. *I wonder if this little one will eat any of this?* he mused. The dragon baby sniffed at the bowl with the vegetables in it, then looked at Jason.

"I don't know if you understand what I am saying but I will tell you anyway. You have to learn how to chew your food little one, like this."

He took a piece of carrot from the bowl and took a bite, chewing it before he swallowed. The dragon took a piece of carrot and began chewing, numerous teeth visible as it did so. When that was finished the little one went to the bowl with the meat and without hesitation began eating, swallowing the chunks of meat whole as it had the first time.

Jason laughed. "Well, I believe you did understand me, but I guess chewing takes too much time, huh?"

Over the next two weeks a list of possible names was compiled. The dragon slept four hours, ate, then went back to sleep. The Sorcerers took shifts meeting its needs. It didn't seem to be growing much except for its wings, which were now more in proportion to its body than they had been.

Jacky and Tara had regained the use of their magic, to everyone's relief, and were eager to continue exercising to rebuild their physical strength and the muscle mass that the trip from Orighen had taken from them. Once the excitement of the baby dragon had subsided everyone except Jason went out to the barn with Jacky and Tara to see if they could identify the owners of the six bundles Brian and Louise had been guarding on Vancouver Island. Jason and the others had memories from their dreams, but because of the turmoil Richard, Midnight and the other Sorcerers endured from them being sent to Earth, and the effects from the virus, those memories were hazy. Most of the memories from their predecessors were clear, however, there were those that were not.

Tara might be able to verify the names Jason and the others had placed on the individual bundles. Jacky was not there at the last battle so she may not be of much help.

"My memories of that day are clear; however, my attention was focused on my own fight. When Richard thrust his sword into Tay'Ron's chest, Tay'Ron's outrage brought all eyes to bear on him," said Tara.

Jacky walked around the tables looking at the items on each. "The swords and knives of each Sorcerer were unique to them. This table holds the Sorcerer Cheryl's items." She picked a scabbard up and pulled the sword out. "This sword belonged to Richard. They were crafted by an elven blacksmith, see how the hilts of swords and knives match."

"That is why you were chosen as our queen, Jacky. The one thing that was always constant, this one is Liam's, that one is

Pam's, that one is Valla's, and that one is Joanne's." Tara pointed to the bundles as she spoke.

———•◦◦❖◦◦•———

The little dragon nudged Jason's leg as he looked out the kitchen window watching Jacky and the others going to the barn. He looked down to see the baby dragon had finished its meal. Instead of letting it go back to sleep this time, Jason coaxed it out the back door with a tidbit of meat. The dragon looked around at the green grass and the different kinds of trees. The sun was shining and there were a few fluffy clouds floating by. A fence at the back of the yard had several bird feeders, each one for a specific kind of bird. Sparrows, chickadees, swallows, blue and Steller's jays, and the elusive hummingbird.

Jason was caught off guard when the baby dragon jumped into the air, spread its wings, and glided toward the back-yard fence. It crash landed short of the fence, doing a summersault and a bit of a skid before it was able to right itself. It sat there watching the birds. The dragon's head went from side to side as birds left or came in to feed.

Jason watched the little one, wondering if it might try catching one of the birds. As he watched he noticed that the blue hide of the dragon with its white spots looked very much likes the blue sky and its puffy white clouds.

Sky would be a fitting name for our little dragon.

Jason heard the others coming back from the barn and went to meet them. "Were you able to confirm our matches of the bundles to the six original Sorcerers?"

Jacky smiled at him as she had been doing more often lately. The looks they gave each other were hard to mistake for anything other than love.

"We did, and we also placed a plaque on each table to honor their memory. We believed that they died that day on Orighen.

We will bring the plaques with us when you find a way to get us home, and we will have to set the record straight."

Jason noticed the change in her voice when she talked about those that had been lost so long ago. He liked her a lot more than he believed he had a right to. He took a deep breath and composed himself.

"Our baby dragon is out watching the birds feeding. I was just waiting for it to try catching one. Notice how the hide on our little one resembles the sky above. Maybe Sky would be a more appropriate name than those we have compiled? It fits well whether it's a boy or a girl."

Everyone was looking at the dragon, most of them nodding in agreement.

"It looks like Sky wins out. All we have to do is get the little one used to the name." Bobby Joe smiled.

The dragon spread its wings, and flapping them up and down, like the birds it was watching, it lifted off the ground a few feet then settled down again. Sky did this several times before turning and walking back to where the Sorcerers were standing. Sky looked at them with what could only be described as a grin.

<I like the name Sky. It feels right to me, and because it will be my name consider my naming process done. You have all been fretting over that subject for days now.>

Jaws dropped and eyes opened wide as Sky's voice was heard in their minds. Sky was talking to them in English, not to mention the fact that *she*—the voice was most definitely female—was talking to them at all.

"You are only two weeks old! How do you have such a firm command of our language?" Samantha asked.

<It took me until now to master your language. A dragon learns some things very quickly. A dragon is born with a basic knowledge of dragon lore, dragon values, and other qualities that only a dragon can have. We learn the rest from the other dragons

in the Dragon Home. I don't see any other dragons here so that makes you my family, and my teachers.>

Sky looked at them one by one to make sure they understood her.

<Sky, my name is Midnight. I preserved this Sanctuary to protect those living here. We would all be in grave danger if it were known that beings with the gift of magic lived here, a place that they can't see. You are a dragon and there are no other dragons here because this is not your world. If anyone outside of this compound sees you, they will come looking for you, to capture you.> Midnight looked at the young dragon as sternly as a cat could. <You need to stay within the magical boundaries I have set to protect us all. Do you understand this, Sky?>

<I would never put my family in danger, Midnight. Show me these boundaries and I will stay within them.> Sky looked at the black cat sitting on the top step of the walkway that surrounded the building.

<I am tired and should rest for a while.> Sky walked to the bottom of the steps and using her powerful hind legs she sprang into the air and, with a couple of flaps of her wings, landed right beside Midnight.

"Well that was unexpected," Marie said as they watched the dragon enter the house. "I didn't see any of this coming so soon, and to think that we have answers to some of our questions is a bonus."

Jason walked toward the back fence watching the birds as they came in to feed or left to let another feed.

"You remind me of him you know. You look somewhat like Richard, your actions are also much the same as his used to be. I know you are not him, but you're here, now," Jacky said as she walked up beside Jason.

"It sounds like you knew him well and it sounds like the two of you had something special. I may not always say what I am thinking, but I am sure that a woman as intelligent as you are sees much more than most." Jason turned and looked at the beautiful strawberry-blonde.

"Perhaps I do. From the way you talk it seems that I have not judged you wrongly," Jacky said. "I know you are not the same man I loved those many years ago, but you are in a way, part him and part you—that is who I am falling in love with now. It doesn't look like I am going back to my world any time soon. Do we make the best of the time we have or not? Unless there is a war going on somewhere I don't know about. That's how I lost my last love."

Jason's answer was straight to the point. He took her in his arms and planted a kiss on her lips. A kiss that lasted much longer than he intended. When they parted Jason asked as he tried to catch his breath. "Should we tell the others?"

Jacky let a slow breath out. "I think they already know." She looked back toward the house and everyone was watching them.

That night Jacky sat up in bed, unable to get the kiss out of her head, nor the feeling of joy it woke inside her. She was trying to get her nerve up to go down to Jason's apartment. She looked over at Tara, who was sleeping soundly. Jacky slipped out of the bed quietly, not wanting to wake Tara, and put her slippers on. She donned her house coat and crept out of the room.

It was not midnight yet as she walked down the stairs. Jacky stopped at the bottom, thinking that this was a mistake. She turned and put one foot on the bottom stair and stopped again. She closed her eyes and turned back around. When she was outside Jason's door, she stopped yet again, pacing back and forth for a minute or two before knocking.

"Come in. It's unlocked."

Jacky entered the room just as Jason got up from his chair. The book lay opened on the table in front of him. He turned and looked at her.

"I have been sitting here for two hours thinking of you. I didn't know how I was going to see you. You share a room with your sister, which makes it awkward for me to come to you."

173

Jacky walked toward him as she opened the house coat she wore and let it slide from her shoulders to the floor. She was completely naked. Without saying a word, she started to undo the buttons of his shirt. He looked at her, watching as she took his clothes off. Jacky was as beautiful without her clothes as she was dressed. When she finished with his clothing, she put her arms around his neck, pressing her body against his. Like an explosion of emotion and passion bundled into one, their sexual desires rose as their lips met for the second time. The chemistry was already there, and Jason picked Jacky up and took her to his bed as he placed a spell to soundproof his rooms. Quite some time later they lay in Jason's bed, their bodies slick with perspiration.

"That was worth waiting for. So, what happens now?" Jacky asked when her breathing slowed to the point where she could talk.

"We already know where we are, Jacky. We have been dancing around this ever since you and Tara woke up. We both made it clear that we are in love and that is not going to change as far as I am concerned. Our love is unconditional. It does not matter to me whether you chose to stay here in my apartment or with your sister. From here, we decide how we proceed, what is best for us, and it does not matter what anyone else thinks."

Jacky hugged him tighter. "If you find a way to send Tara and me back home, all this will end. I have a responsibility to the people of Geldania. I am their queen. I cannot abandon them, even for love. Tara and I believe that our country is being run by Sorcerers from the southern continent and that cannot be allowed to continue any longer than it has to."

"There is nothing to keep me here, on this world Jacky," Jason said. "The others are capable of taking care of themselves now. Sky is from your world as well, we believe, and even if she is not, there are at least dragons living on your world, and she has a right to live with her own kind. Of course, that is only if we can find a way to get back to your world."

Jacky moved over top of Jason, straddling him, hands on the bed on either side of him. "My world. All of you were given the gift of someone from my world, which in part makes it your world as well. I believe the answer is in that book of yours, that you will find it someday, and we can return home to battle those who would try and rule us again." Jacky pressed her lips to his before he could say anything else. Their sexual urges reignited, and their lust for each other prevailed.

When they woke in the morning Jacky pointed out that all she had to wear was her housecoat.

"You can make that housecoat into anything you want it to be, something that pleases you, so I do not see your problem. There is something I think you should know about me before we leave my room. When Midnight found me, I was ninety years old and had only a few months left to live. Too many people knew of this and changing my physical self was my only option, so Midnight and I faked the death of DeWayne, my former self, and I became Jason. Of course, I am still the same person I was, I have only changed my appearance."

Jason changed into DeWayne, to show Jacky what he looked like before.

"What were you like before you met Midnight?"

Jason changed back. "I was a tradesman all my adult life and worked until I couldn't. I lost the love of my life soon after we were married. I never found anyone who could take her place, not that I didn't try. When I became ill everything changed, I stopped trying."

"It sounds like you have a lot of time to make up for," Jacky said, smiling.

Laughing, they went for breakfast.

—◦◦◦❦◦◦◦—

Summer was slipping away, and fall would be upon them in another month. Sky continued to watch the birds in the back yard. These birds were not dragons, but they did fly, so technically she should be able to learn from them. Sky was getting the hang of it. Taking off and flying seemed to come naturally, landing on the other hand took some getting used to. She knew she would get better with practice, so she began flying for longer periods each time she went out. Sky was taking her time trying not to overdo it with her flying. Eventually she managed to get her landing under control too.

Sky was also learning how to use a computer. She used magic to turn it on and off, as well as to type in her searches and for scrolling up and down. She wanted to learn about this world, the dangers Jason told her about, and all the interesting accomplishments the people of Earth had made over time.

The first week of September Sky had a growth spurt, which created a problem navigating in close quarters. She wasn't that big and could get in and out of the house easily enough, but it didn't matter how careful she was, her tail seemed to have a mind of its own and things got knocked over and broken.

Sky suggested that she move out to the barn. She had been out there on many occasions and knew there was much more room there than in the house, and she could go flying any time she chose, too. Sky didn't have an issue with the animals already housed there. Only time would tell if they had an issue with her.

CHAPTER 17

UNEXPECTED VISITORS

On Sky's first night in the barn she discovered she wasn't the only one sharing the barn with the livestock. Two other creatures entered the barn in the early morning, just as the sky outside was beginning to lighten.

<Good morning, Jason and Jacky.> Sky greeted them when they entered the barn that morning to take care of chores. <Two foxes have made a den in the hay bin, and they both have the gift. Could they have hitched a ride home from Vancouver Island?>

Jason frowned. "Really Sky, are you sure about this? We were occupied with other things at the time, so I suppose that two small creatures could have stowed away on the motorhome without anyone noticing. Where are these two now Sky?"

<They are in the hay bin sleeping. They did seem to be a bit on the skinny side. Maybe Brian and Louise know something about these two. If they are from the island, then those two should know them, or know of them.>

Jason scanned the hay bin. "They seem to be comfortable Sky. We will talk to Brian and Louise once we have finished our chores. They may have forgotten something like that during their transition to human, or they didn't think it was important. But they are the best choice for communicating with the foxes."

Breakfast was ready when they arrived back at the house, so Jason and Jacky sat down at the table and loaded their plates before sharing the news.

"Brian, I have a question for you," Jason said. "Sky discovered two foxes with the gift of sorcery sleeping in the barn. She thought they may have come home with us from Vancouver Island, so I wondered if you or Louise might know something about them."

Brian looked at Louise. "I do remember them now that you mentioned them. Louise?"

Louise frowned, looking at Jason. "Yes. I do remember them. They always were a little skittish and fled when the meteor landed." She paused as the memories returned. "When Midnight made us guardians, those two were hiding in a bush right behind us, so Midnight's spell must have included them as well. Brian and I slept on the place where the Sorcerers buried the bundles. The two foxes slept there too. We spent part of the night together. Wolves and foxes hunt at night, so part of our night was spent looking for food. Then we slept for part of the day while Brian was out looking for food."

Brian added, "They must have been watching from the woods and followed us when we went to the motorhome, then found some place to hide before we left. That is the only thing that makes sense. How else could they have come here?"

Jason smiled; they had learned something new today. It appeared that the transition from animal to human had an some effect on memory, although a minor one. "I can't argue with your reasoning Brian. I think they would be better off living with us. What do you think? Are we going to be able to convince them to make the change? They have been here as long as the two of you have and they haven't made their presence known."

"They know Brian and me, so I think it would be best if we went out to the barn to see if we can talk to them."

"They are sleeping in the barn for the time being. Maybe our best chance of talking to them would be when they wake to hunt this evening. You say they are skittish; do you think there is going to be a challenge trying to convince them with words? I suppose we could set a trap as a last resort," Bobby Joe said, looking around the table.

<I think you should just leave some food for them by their den, where they sleep, and try to gain their trust. Remember they are still wild creatures regardless of their gift. Brian and Louise have already been in their shoes so they would have a better chance as a bear and a wolf. I remember someone saying that you catch more flies with honey than vinegar. These two are afraid. Trusting humans is going to take convincing—not force.> Sky added her two cents just to let them know she was listening too.

Jason laughed. "Well Sky, you just solved our problem. Does anyone have anything to add? Brian and Louise, we'll leave it to you two to convince the stowaways to trust us."

Brian and Louise agreed and left to consult with Sky.

Jason went back to reading the book, but it seemed that the more he read the more there was—the number of pages left to read seemed to be growing rather than shrinking. He was sure that it was just his active imagination playing tricks on him. Some of what he read they already knew; some was new information that he shared with the others. Why everyone called them spells he did not know. They were just ideas that one could picture in one's mind, then use magic to make them real. The book explained things with more detail than Midnight; however, it did not give the reader everything.

Summer was coming to an end. Fall brought colder nights and not much warmth during the day. Of course, snow could be coming any day now as well. Brian and Louise were in the barn hoping to communicate with the two foxes. Convincing them that they were not going to be harmed and that they had the ability to change into human form was going to take some doing due to their skittish nature.

Brian and Louise placed a small amount of food close by the hay bin so the two foxes would have no trouble finding it when they woke. When Brian and Louise sensed the foxes were waking, they approached the bin from opposite sides. Louise turned into her wolf form.

<I see you hitched a ride when you saw we were leaving. Don't be frightened. I only want to talk to you,> Louise said as the foxes' noses appeared, obviously smelling the food.

The pair of foxes cringed, trying to blend in with the hay that was close at hand. Their white fur against the straw-colored hay made that almost impossible. Louise approached them. <Help yourself to the food while we talk. You can come with us to the house where it is warm. There is more food there and the people won't hurt you. This is something you should think about before you answer.>

The two foxes stopped eating to look at each other. <What if we refuse to go with you?> one of them said.

<If you refuse, we will leave you alone. However, all the holes in the barn will be repaired and you will have to find a new den for the winter. We can do no more here, Brian. Let us return to our nice—warm—house.>

Brian, in his bear form, stepped into their line of vision. <We have slept side by side for thousands of years little ones. You saw us change into human form and I presume that scared you. You are like our family, and we only want to help. Louise and I will not let anything happen to you, you have our word.>

Brian and Louise changed into their human forms. <It's not so bad being like this and you can join us.> They turned to leave.

<We will go with you,> one of the foxes said.

Brian and Louise picked up their two fellow, accidental, guardians and headed back to the house.

The rest of the household were just about finished the evening meal when Brian and Louise came into the common room, each holding a fox with long white fur.

"They say they need time to think about changing to human form," Brian said out loud and telepathically. "But I think they are just stalling to get free food."

Marie stood up, a smile on her face. "Frank and I should check them to make sure they are healthy. We wouldn't want to find out that they have some kind of unknown disease, now would we?"

It was clear that Marie had something in mind as she guided Brian and Louise into the kitchen with their charges. Marie and Frank took a couple of bowls out and used magic to fill them with chunks of cooked beef and gravy. Marie placed them on the floor while Brian and Louise put the foxes down.

"The longer these two put off changing from their fox persona into human form, the longer they will have to wait to learn how to make their own food." Marie winked at the other humans. "What do you think, Louise?"

"There is that, and let's not forget that they will have their own room here in the house where it's nice and warm in the wintertime. What do you think, Frank?"

"They come from Vancouver Island where it is reasonably warm in the winter. I think rooms upstairs, here in the cold Alberta winters, is worth the change."

Brian again played conciliator, apparently speaking to the humans but his words were meant for the foxes. "When Jason asked me to change into the human form, I was afraid of what that meant for me. How was I going to fit in with other humans? How was I going to hunt for my food? How was I going to communicate? The transition was much easier than Louise and I expected it would be. Everyone here made us feel like part of this family."

The four humans returned to the common room. Jason looked up from the book. "Do I want to know?"

Frank shrugged his shoulders. "Marie gave them some roast beef with a bit of gravy, and we chatted for a bit. Nothing intrusive I assure you. However, tanning their hind ends did cross my mind."

When their guests were finished their meal, they came into the common room and went to sleep by the fire. "What can you tell us about these two Brian? Louise? Everything you can think of."

Louise cleared her throat. "I believe they came from the same litter and they are both female. Sisters, twin sisters I suppose. We really don't know any more than that; foxes pretty much keep to themselves."

Jason smiled at her. "They are female. They would respond better to other females I would think. Jacky, you are a diplomat; perhaps you could join Louise, Marie, and the others in this endeavor. See what you can do to convince them that the change is to their benefit. We can't let them wander around the way they are. The gift is already active in them as it was with Louise and Brian. If they figure out how to use it…"

"You make sense," Jacky said. "It is time for a woman to woman talk with our new guests."

The two foxes woke near midnight and went into the kitchen, where they had found food earlier. There were two bowls with meat, vegetables, and gravy by the table. Louise stood up from the chair where she was sitting and knelt by the two.

"You will come with me when you are finished eating. The other women of the house, and I, would like to sit down and have a girl-to-girl talk with you."

All the women living at the Sanctuary knew how to change into wolves, eagles, and bears. The fox was a miniature wolf—the differences were 'cosmetic.' Foxes, wolves, dogs, and dingoes are all related as they are all members of the Canidae family of carnivores. Louise had explained that the fox's body structure was the same as hers.

When Louise and the foxes returned to the common room, the men had retired for the night. "Sit down and let's talk," Louise said to the foxes.

The human women, each wearing a housecoat, sat in a circle around the two foxes.

"We know your story," Jacky said. "You were watching when the bear and the wolf changed into their human forms. We also know that when Midnight gave those two a spell to increase their life span you somehow received it too. Like Louise, your wolf, and Brian, your bear, you have a gift. You can change yourselves into the female human form you chose as they did. I know that you're scared.

"There are advantages in becoming human. You will be a part of our family. You will learn how to use your powers of sorcery properly. You will never go hungry, and you will always be warm. Life here is not all work. We have time to ourselves, or we can get together with others and enjoy learning different tasks together. Now is the time for you to help yourselves."

<How long is this going to take?> one of them asked.

"That depends on the two of you," Louise replied.

<Then let us get started.>

"We will show you how to change from your present forms to that of the human form," Jacky said. "After that you will begin your lessons on how to speak, look after yourselves, how to use tools to help you learn, and finally how to use your gift of magic. Do you have any questions?"

The women removed their housecoats so the twin foxes could see that not all women were the same. The transformation took longer than expected. It wasn't because the foxes didn't understand what to do, but because they were not happy with the results. When the transformations were complete, two six-foot-tall women stood where the two foxes had stood moments before. Both had silver hair that fell to their waists. The eyes of an adult fox are yellow, and it seemed that these two wished to keep that eye color. It was strange to see at first, but everyone got used to it after a while.

Like Brian and Louise, changing into human form was all they had to do for now. Once the two human-foxes were dressed they were shown to an empty room upstairs. "Brian and I are in the next room," said Louise.

Louise, Samantha, and Susan took on the project of helping the two silver-haired women learn to speak the English language. They also showed them female names. One chose Pia, and the other one chose Petra. Samantha studied the two trying to find something that would tell them apart, a distinguishing feature. She noticed that Pia had a hairline scar under her left eye that was almost imperceptible unless you were looking for it. For now, she kept that to herself.

Louise and Susan decided that teaching Pia and Petra how to use a computer was a good next step. Once the demonstration on using the device was complete, they showed them how to access the internet to find knowledge.

They had a light snow fall a few days after Pia and Petra had made the transition into their human form. Fall was the season when the weather changed in the blink of an eye. This close to the mountains it wasn't unusual to have snow this early and it might be gone in a couple of days. Of course, Sky had never seen snow, so she spent hours frolicking in the white, fluffy crystals. Watching her reminded Jason of the first and only pet his former self had had. Ranger was a border collie and happen to be the runt of the litter. The young DeWayne could not let the little one be put down, so he talked the breeder in to letting him take the pup. When Ranger saw his first snowfall his reaction was much the same as Sky's.

One of the highlights of his past, a different life almost forgotten.

CHAPTER 18

UNKNOWN FACTORS

Jason glared at the book. He read hundreds of pages every day, and although he was acquiring new knowledge that was pertinent to their learning growth, he was still disappointed. He got up from his chair and paced back and forth.

They could have put a table of contents at the beginning like a normal book. At least then I would know where to start. There must be an easier way—something I am not seeing.

He shook his head at his thoughts, put the book down and walked away. Jacky and Tara asking him daily if he had found anything yet wasn't helping his mood.

Jacky and Tara began training their new family on Earth the way they trained on Orighen. The proper way to fight with a sword was Tara's strong point. Jacky showed them different techniques for throwing a knife and how to use a bow and arrows. Both Tara and Jacky also had their own version of hand-to-hand combat. When Bobby Joe and Amanda showed them the Earth version, they discovered that the two were similar in some ways. Jacky took the best from both and they began learning a new, improved version.

A month had passed when Tara and Jacky planned a friendly competition for them. The winner of each event would get a gold coin from the stash of coins recovered from the six bundles. Jacky and Tara would judge four categories: knife throwing, hand-to-hand combat, sword play, and archery. This was a one-on-one competition, putting siblings and friends against each other. They began early in the morning out by the barn. Sky was excited. She had read about tournaments and now she had a front row seat.

In the knife throwing, Pia surprised them all by taking first place easily. Brian took first place in hand-to-hand combat, partly because of his size, although he was well versed in martial arts. Susan was the winner in the sword play competition. And Jason took first place in the archery competition. They celebrated the winners with a feast and a party that lasted well into the night. The next morning there were a few imagined hangovers, as alcohol had no effect on them. They laughed and joked about the competition and the festivities throughout breakfast.

"I have always considered my skill at knife throwing to be above average, Pia. I bow to you as the new champion," Samantha said.

"I owe my skill to your teaching Samantha," Pia replied.

The banter continued as Jason picked the book up and went to his room. He set the book on the pedestal, sat in his chair and glared at it.

In a moment of frustration, he reached out and touched the book.

"Take me to the traveling spell."

To his surprise the pages began turning. Jason stared at the page he had unearthed when the pages stopped: it was what he had been looking for all these months. The spell was, in itself, simple. The only problem was, they needed a visual picture of the place they wanted to go.

Picking the book up, he rushed to the common room yelling. "I found it! I found it! I found a way to get you back to Orighen! All we need is a place for you to go to. It has to be a precise image. Any deviation and you could end up on Julina."

"Where is Julina?" Jacky asked confused.

"It's nowhere, it doesn't exist. The point is you need to give a positively accurate description of the place you want to end up at, like the barn."

Jacky looked at Tara. "We are going to need some time alone to think this through. It should be a remote place, some place where there is a small chance that anyone, or anything, will interfere with our arrival."

Jason nodded.

<This means that Jacky and Tara were sent to a specific place. And suggests that others from the southern continent have been to Earth, just like Tay'Ron. Did he bring the book here or was it someone else? I doubt he left Sky's egg here.> Midnight gave them all something to think about.

Jacky and Tara had shared their story with their new friends so Jason knew they were not sisters, biologically, but the two were raised together. Tara's mother, Julia, was the woman who cooked and cleaned for Jacky's family. Tara was born two weeks before Jacky and because Talia, Jacky's mother, could not breastfeed—she was unable to produce enough breastmilk—Julie took over feeding Jacky. When a southern raiding party was spotted coming their way, Talia instructed Julia and two of the ranch guards to take the children and go to the safe place they kept for emergencies in the mountains.

Jorden, Julia's mate, was one of those guards. The safe place was half a day's travel from the ranch. Six farmers and ranchers had built the retreat over the years because of the rise in raiders attacking outlying homes. When Julia, Jorden, Dell, and the babies arrived at the caves, others were already there. They were told that the raiders had slaughtered their families and their guards as well. Jacky and Tara grew up together as sisters. They started learning how to use their gift and how to defend themselves at an early age. Jason recalled the story as he watched the two women move to another table.

Jacky and Tara retreated to a corner of the common room.

"I am the brawn, and you are the brains of this family," said Tara. "We have had little time to travel together over our lifetime so there are only a half-dozen places we have been to together, and there is only one of those that we know well enough to be able to draw a picture of. A place we can be sure there will be little chance of anyone, or anything, being there to interfere with our arrival. The Dragon Home in the eastern mountains would be the best place, although it has been many winters since we were there together. The people who live there rarely go up to the cavern."

Jacky nodded and went to the writing table to get a large pad and two pencils. "We both draw the cavern the way we remember it, and then we compare our drawings and go from there. Either one of us may remember something the other didn't. As Jason said this needs to be absolute, no mistakes, or we may end up in a place called limbo that I read about. We will be of no use to Geldania if we die trying to get home."

When they compared their drawings at the end of the day, there were some differences. Jason suggested they photocopy each drawing to a transparent plastic and overlay them. That allowed them to come up with something they both agreed on. They showed it to the others.

<I have noticed that no one has asked for my input on this subject,> Sky interjected. <It seems that you are only interested in getting Tara and Jacky back to Orighen. That is my home too, and I would like to go on this journey as well, to a place where I am not the only dragon.>

Jason had to laugh at the contempt in Sky's voice. "Maybe we should all look at the future that awaits us here. We are prisoners here in our Sanctuary. This is our place of solitude where no one can harm us, but out there we have to hide our true nature. We are slaves to our new abilities. If we were to go to Orighen we would be like any other Sorcerer. No one there would want to strap us to an operating table so they can find out what makes us tick, or worse, try and take it from us."

The others frowned looking at each other.

"Are you asking us to consider going to a world we know very little about—other than our dreams and what Jacky and Tara have told us of Orighen. That's a lot to ask, don't you think?" Amanda wasn't sure if she was looking for support or for a solid reason to go with Jacky, Tara, and Sky.

Jason was direct. "Between our dreams, and what Jacky and Tara have told us about Orighen, I feel I know Geldania pretty well. Each of us will need to make our own choice, but think about the options you have here, and compare them to the chances you have there. I am going with them. If you haven't noticed, Jacky and I are in love and I am not going to lose that now."

Susan looked around the table. "Samantha and I don't have any reason to stay here, but we will sit down and discuss the matter. Maybe the rest of you should do the same."

"It is going to take a week or two for us to get things in order before we can leave," said Adam.

Midnight stood in front of Jason. He bent over and picked her up, resting her in his lap.

<I am very tired my friend. I think my time is almost up. I won't be going with you. Tell me you understand.>

Jason gently stroked the cat's head. <Are you sure about this Midnight? If there is a chance that you can be cured once we get to Orighen, wouldn't you want to take that chance?>

<No, Jason. My time in this life is almost done. There is no cure here, nor on Orighen. The book tells you that it isn't from Orighen, so I would have to presume that Tay'Ron wasn't either, and you haven't found anything in the book relating to this virus, or any other. The trip there would surely finish me anyway. I am content with my lot. I will not be going with you.>

Jason choked back the tears that tried to escape his eyes. <All right my dear friend I will not pressure you. We will leave you to look after this place just in case we decide to come back someday.>

Midnight jumped down and went to the chair she usually slept in and allowed Jason to lift her on to it.

Jason could feel it right down to his bones, the dread of losing another friend. Midnight was his one real connection to the gift he now possessed. She had made him who he was today, and regardless of her strict teaching method, and the vague explanations she gave him, he would miss her dearly. From faking his death, to re-designing the Sanctuary, to teaching a new band of Sorcerers, they had been through a lot together.

Jason pushed that thought to the back of his mind in order to concentrate on the matter at hand. *I have already committed to leaving here and going there, so now I ought to put my affairs in order. What will we need when we get there? What can we take with us when we leave here? How much, if any, of our life here can we share once we get there? So many questions but no answers, yet.*

Over the next three days Jason heard from all the others at the Sanctuary. They all decided that, because they had no living relatives here, there was no reason why they could not leave Earth and go to a place where they would be welcome for who they were now.

Jason called a meeting in the common room. "I have thought about this for several days now. We could trade our paper money for gold and silver. From the pouches we found in the bundles we retrieved from Vancouver Island we know those two precious metals are also found on Orighen. Adam, your accounting knowledge might be helpful as we do this."

Adam nodded.

"We also should decide what we can and cannot bring with us. Cell phones, computers, and any other kind of technology must stay here. If you have memories you wish to keep, like photos, print them out, but you should keep them to yourselves, no sharing with those we meet there. I believe that two weeks should be enough time to accomplish this."

"Two weeks isn't much time for what you're asking," Adam said. "Liquidating our accounts and turning that into gold and silver is going to take time. There are only so many shops that handle those metals."

"That is a good point. I intend to purchase a couple of kilograms of each and donate the rest of my estate to charities I deal with," Jason said. "Anyone else?"

Jason could tell them where to find all the gold they would need, but decided to remain silent. On one of his excursions while refurbishing the Sanctuary he discovered he could sense the precious metal as he followed the stream that provided water to the buildings. The intent of one of those excursions had been to find where the stream originated. He knew about metals, including the precious ones. As he walked along the bank of the stream he sensed the presence of gold. The stream's origin was underground, and it flowed through a vein of gold, which deposited the gold he sensed in the stream. If it came down to it, he would tell the others, but he doubted he would have to. However, things didn't always go as planned. Like Midnight, he decided to keep this secret to himself, for now.

Jacky spoke in Geldanian. "Since we are all going, I think we should speak Geldanian whenever we are in the Sanctuary. That will give you all practice and make slips into English less likely once we arrive on Orighen."

Jason found homes for the animals and fowl on farms he had visited in the past. It only took eight days for everyone to return with both gold and silver ingots. They had gone into the city in twos and threes to settle their affairs. Jason had set the money still coming in from *The Invasion of Geldania* to go into a trust fund to support up and coming writers, donated all his apartment furniture to a company that would ensure those in need received it at no cost to them, and cancelled his lease. All ties to Earth had been severed.

As they sat by the fire in the common room making their plans to leave, Midnight approached. She jumped up on the coffee table in the center of the sitting room. She looked at them one by one.

<I have done what I set out to do and had several surprises in doing so. One of those was finding out that the Sorcerer's magic and mine became mixed together, so all of you have a unique form of magic that you will have to figure out as you grow. It is time for me to leave you. This is my last gift to each of you.>

A blue glow surrounded her and began to swirl. Midnight was lost in that light. Suddenly the light broke into fifteen separate balls and without pause one glowing blue ball entered each one of them. Midnight had just become a part of them. No one spoke, no one moved. Then the tears fell freely. A long cry came from the barn. Sky was grieving the loss of a good friend as well.

Time seemed to stand still until Jason broke the silence. "I don't think any of us were prepared for what just happened. Midnight was family, and although she told us on more than one occasion that her time was growing shorter each day, we were not listening to how she said it. I cannot say what the glowing blue ball of energy she gave to each of us is, or what it will do to us, but I suppose we will find the answer to that question in time."

"There is nothing more we can do now. We have other things to tend to." Jacky wasn't being callous, she was being practical. This was the second time she had had to grieve Midnight's loss.

The next two days were spent packing what they wanted to bring. Everyone had to memorize the picture Jacky and Tara put together illustrating the place they would be going. High in the mountains along the eastern coast of Geldania was the Dragon Home. Even higher yet was the huge cavern where the dragons lived. The cavern had two entrances from the outside. Only a dragon could access those tunnels from the outside.

It took the better part of the day for everyone to commit the detailed image to memory. A hallway led to the stairs that went to the lower levels where the humans lived. From that hallway a short wall about four feet high and three feet wide ran for one hundred feet. The cavern wall was another hundred or so feet beyond that on one side. There were two large corridors on the other side of the cavern. One across from the hall that led to the stairs. The other was at the far end of the cavern visible only by a faint light. Along the wall between those corridors were large holes, or maybe caves. What these were for they did not know, and it was irrelevant for the imaging. The floor of the cavern was scarred from dragon talons when they leaped into the air to begin their flight.

Jason took the picture to Sky.

<I know this place. It is a part of my memories, the memories I was born with. This is my home. There is no doubt in my mind that this is where we are going Jason.>

"Perhaps Jacky and Tara should have brought the picture to you instead of me."

"If we leave after sunup there is less of a chance we will be seen. Not that it really matters, we will be gone. But at least the Sanctuary will remain hidden in case we decide to come back here someday." Samantha pointed out.

It was agreed that they would leave shortly after sunrise.

"Everyone should get some rest tonight as we will need to be sharp. We will have to have a decent meal before we go to ensure we have enough energy for the trip. Remember the condition Jacky and Tara were in when they arrived." Marie spoke in her doctor voice.

No one replied. They went to their rooms and tried to rest.

Jason tried to sleep, but thoughts of the trip kept him awake. There were too many variables, too many things that could go wrong. With a great effort he managed to push those thoughts out of his mind and focus on the positive.

Two hours before sunrise Jason went into the kitchen where Susan, Samantha, Pia and Petra were preparing their last meal in the Sanctuary. Brian and Louise came in, followed by Frank and Marie. Jason knew the others would be there soon.

They took their time with breakfast. "What do you think we will find when we get there?" John asked, directing the question to Tara.

"The cavern should be empty, except for us. What may be at the bottom of the stairs we don't know. As far as we know, the southerners might already control the Dragon Home. It has been months since we arrived here," she replied.

Pia scrunched up her face as if she had eaten something sour. "Someone sent you and Jacky here, and I don't think they were friends of yours. So, you're saying we could find ourselves fighting for our lives?"

Jacky looked at Pia and Petra. "I am not going to candy-coat it, and tell you there isn't a possibility that the Dragon Home may have been taken over by an enemy force. However, the people living there would not be easily defeated. The place is a fortress and easy to defend."

"You mentioned earlier that the stairs to the lower level are spiral. We would have quite an advantage over anyone trying to climb those stairs I would think," Bobby Joe said, looking at both Jacky and Tara for an answer.

Tara smiled. "You are sharp Bobby Joe. The shaft that houses the stairs is at least three hundred feet from top to bottom. The stairs are part of the wall. They spiral around the curvature to the bottom. The railing is no more than waist high with supports every ten steps. An arrow travels much further and faster going down than it does going up."

Jason laughed at the nervous banter. A trip of this kind had never been done by anyone sitting there. Jacky and Tara hadn't planned their trip, someone else did that for them. Everyone knew the risk they were about to take. "Maybe we should concentrate on getting there first. We will deal with what we find when we get there."

The laughter that followed was more forced than natural.

Jason expected that, like him, they were experiencing some anxiety. They each put a dozen of the protein and energy bars into their packs. Four wafers wrapped in a banana leaf and tied with string. Everything was prepared for the trip. Sky was just finishing her breakfast too. When the sun came up Jason prompted the others to gather their things.

They walked out to the barn, backpacks in hand. They were dressed in clothes resembling those from the bundles they had retrieved. Each of them donned knife belts and sword belts, and fastened their bows and quivers to their backpacks. Jason picked up his staff, attaching it to his backpack next to his bow. Sky led the way to an open place between the barn and the house.

They formed a circle with Jason holding one of Sky's forearms and Brian the other. Jacky was on Jason's right and Louise on Brian's left. Tara was to Jacky's right. Bobby Joe was to Louise's left and John next to her. Susan and Samantha, Adam and Amanda followed, with Frank, Marie, Pia, and Petra completing the circle. They all formed the picture in their minds of the cavern and thought of Orighen.

Sky took charge of the flow of magic before anyone could say anything. A flash of blue light surrounded all of them, and in an instant, they were gone, leaving a slightly charred open space in front of the barn.

Jason tried to think of something, anything, to stay conscious, but it was a fruitless effort. As he drifted into the void of unconsciousness wondering if this was really going to work, a meteor shot across the sky and vanished into the heavens.

The End of Book 1
Richard B.

GLOSSARY

EARTH

DeWayne: Receives the Sorcerer Richard's gift. MC, old man (89 at start of book), arthritis, lung condition; requires two canes and oxygen via nasal canula; hair and beard to waist.
Becomes Jason Blain.

Midnight: A Furl Cat from Orighen; is a creature of magic with the ability to take the gift from one who is dying and is able to give that gift to one who is alive.

Kristen: Bar tender at DeWayne's favorite bar.

Samantha and Susan: Twin chefs: Father Brad & Mother Alice (died in a car accident 2035); {Sault St. Marie, Ontario} Samantha received the Sorcerer Joanne's gift. Midnight did not take the bond between twins into consideration when she transferred the gift.

Adam and Amanda: Amanda was a business manager and Adam's twin sister. Adam was an accountant. Their parents Philip and Bernice who were killed in an accident caused by a drunk driver. Amanda received the Sorcerer Pam's gift which was also transferred to Adam. {Thunder Bay, Ontario}

Marie and Frank: Doctors: They worked out of their motorhome servicing communities that rarely saw doctors. Marie received the Sorcerer Valla's gift and because of their bond through marriage Frank received it as well. {Vancouver Island, British Columbia}

Bobby Joe: Bobby Joe was head librarian at one of the larger libraries in the city. Her mother, Sue Lin, was from Japan and her father, Jonas, was Norwegian. Midnight gave her the Sorcerer Cheryl's gift. {North Bay, Ontario}

Johnathan: Engineer Johnathan was an only child. His mother, Mauna, was of African descent and his father, Johnathan, was Irish. The gift of Sorcery he received was Liam's. {Ferguson Cove, Nova Scotia}

Paul: Sous Chef at the Rainbow restaurant and bar owned by Susan and Samantha.

Diann: Wife of Paul, Maître d', bookkeeper, and she is in charge of the front-end staff.

Brad: Father of Susan and Samantha who died in a car accident.

Alice: Mother of Susan and Samantha who died in a car accident.

Runner: A timber wolf DeWayne, Samantha and Susan befriended from The Quest.

Luna: Runner's mate.

Azul: A bald eagle DeWayne, Samantha, and Susan befriended from The Quest.

Lima: Azul's mate.

Jakiera: Also known as Jacky, the fifth female Sorcerer to join Richards group of orphan warriors. She became Queen of Geldania and was exiled to Earth approximately three thousand years after the last battle by southern Sorcerers.

Tarisha: Also known as Tara, who became the Admiral of the Queens army. Sister by association to Jakiera who was also exiled to Earth by southern Sorcerers about three thousand years after the last battle. She joined Richard's rebels with her sister.

Sky: A dragon egg found on Earth in the mountains in BC, Sky's egg hatched on Earth and she became part of the family of Sorcerers at the Sanctuary.

Sanctuary aka "Connors Way Station": A secluded place east of the Rocky Mountains that Midnight found and protected with magic for the Sorcerers that would be reborn on Earth; a place where they would be safe from prosecution or worse.

Brian: A bear Midnight chose as a guardian to protect a valuable treasure on Vancouver Island who became a Sorcerer due to the magic items he was guarding.

Louise: A timber wolf, Brian's co-guardian on Vancouver Island also a Sorcerer who becomes his lover after they learn how to change into human form.

Pia and Petra: Two foxes who are accidental guardians of the treasure on Vancouver Island.

ORIGHEN, GELDANIA: PEOPLE, ANIMALS, AND MEASURES:

Geldanian: Someone from Geldania.

Tay'Ron: Evil Sorcerer trying to take over the rule of Orighen.

Richard: A Sorcerer whose family was murdered by the southern raiders. Richard formed a group of other orphaned Sorcerers to battle the invading forces from the south, He was one of six Sorcerers exiled to Earth from Orighen at the last battle.

Bragg: Friend of Richard's whose family was murdered by the southern raiders.

Valaren Ranch: Richard's home.

Chelsea Farm: Bragg's home.

Liam: One of the only two male Sorcerers exiled to Earth by Tay'Ron from Orighen.

George and Delbert: Childhood friends of Liam.

Paltaren: The village where Liam, George, and Delbert lived.

Cheryl: One of four female Sorcerers exiled to Earth by Tay'Ron from Orighen.

Obed Village: The Village where Cheryl lived, all died at the hands of the southerners.

Joanne: A female Sorcerer exiled to Earth from Orighen.

Holden: Where Joanne lived, and all others died at the hands of the southerners.

Pam: The third of four female Sorcerers who were exiled to Earth from Orighen.

Tamara: Pam's older sister.

Farnsworth: The hamlet where Pam was born.

Valla: The fourth of four female Sorcerers sent to Earth from Orighen.

Nora: The town where Valla grew up in.

Scarlet: A dragon on Orighen who disappears during the final battle.

Kolten: large grazing animal eight feet high at the back with four short but powerful legs, weighing over 3,500lbs.

Ranis: A six-legged animal used as a pack animal and transportation.

Kurke: A bird used for food. Six feet tall and weighing up to 325lbs.

metronome: A form of measure on Orighen approximately 1 mile.

metra: A form of measure on Orighen approximately 1 foot.

centra: A form of measure on Orighen approximately 1 inch.

gama: A form of weight measure on Orighen approximately 1 pound.

gorma: A form of weight measure on Orighen approximately 1 ounce.

helecna: A form of time on Orighen approximately 1 second.

helcna: A form of time on Orighen approximately 1 minute.

hecna: A form of time on Orighen approximately 1 hour.

heclona: A form of time on Orighen approximately 1 month.

One winter: A form of time on Orighen approximately 1 year.

ABOUT THE AUTHOR

Rick (Richard B.) Ogle was born in 1951 in Northern Ontario. This is his first appearance in the writing world. He worked for forty-five plus years as a journeyman fabricator/welder. In 1978 Rick wrote a short story titled "Storms" that turned into two books. His work always came first, so writing took the back burner. Writing of *Sorcerers Reborn* began in late 2000, but again work came first, so the book was not revisited until he was forced into retirement in 2013.

In 1998 Rick went back to school to learn something that would get him out of his chosen trade as a fabricator/welder. In 1999 he spent six months as an adult literacy tutor and found that was rewarding when he saw the progress each student was making. He currently holds an Adult Instructors Diploma. He completed a six-month course to obtain an A+ computer technicians' certification. He has an AutoCAD certificate in drafting and design. He instructed classes for Microsoft Word, Excel, PowerPoint, and Access at the North Cariboo Community Skills Center in Quesnel BC.

Rick is self-taught in HTML (Hyper Text Markup Language) code and built his website in 1998 while he was in school. He named his website "Poems and Short Stories by Richard B". That website is still going today. Home page URL: http://www.richardbees.ca